Heavenly Realm Publishing
Houston, Texas

Published by, Heavenly Realm Publishing
PO Box 682532
Houston, TX 77268
1-866-216-0696

Visit our Website at: www.heavenlyrealmpublishing.com

Printed in the United States of America

ISBN—13- 978-1-937911-97-3 (soft cover)
ISBN—13-978-1-937911-98-0 (hard cover)
ISBN—13-978-1-937911-99-7 (ebook)

Library of Congress Control Number—2016934375
Silent and Still/ LaJohna Newbould

This book is printed on acid free paper.

Printed in the United States of America

Unless otherwise indicated, all scriptures quotations in this book are from the King James Version of the Holy Bible, and NIV version.

SILENT
and Still

A novel

LaJohna Newbould

Dedications

I dedicate this book to God the Father, God the Son and God the Holy Spirit. For without Him this book would not have been written. It continually amazes me what an awesome God I serve and I thank Him for all He has done for me.

To The Readers

Whether or not you choose to believe in Jesus, is a choice given to you by that same Jesus. He gave it to you by paying a debt He did not owe. Your debt. But because that debt has been paid, you are given free will. The free will to believe in Him or not to believe in Him. It is your choice.

Table of Contents

Prologue

"Well! Well! Well! Lookie here!" The man thought to himself not wanting to take his eyes off of Chloe. "Long time no see."

He hadn't wanted to bring his cousin's teenage daughter to the mall today, but they had both pestered him until he had finally given in and said yes and then it was just to get them off his back. And now—well now, he was mighty glad he did.

He continued to watch Seth and Chloe as their eyes scanned the food court looking for a place to sit. As luck would have it, Chloe spotted a table not far from him. She got Seth's attention and they both started walking in his direction, oblivious to the threat that was so close. Chloe sat down while at the same time lightly pushing the packages she had been carrying underneath the table.

"Chloe, are you sure you want to do this? Seth asked, looking at her with compassion. His thoughts couldn't help but return to the time when Chloe's stalking began.

"Yes, Seth, I am sure. We have to do it sometime and it might as well be now."

"Okay. If you think you're ready. You want your usual, right?"

"Right."

While Seth was gone, the man continued to watch Chloe. From his table, he could see both her and Seth at the same time. He kept an eye on Seth, but he mainly wanted to watch Chloe.

Seth went directly to Chloe's favorite Mexican place, Casa Ole. After picking up their order, he immediately returned to their table thankful it had not taken him very long. He didn't want to leave Chloe alone any longer than he had to. Not here and not now.

"Thanks, Seth. You know how much I like Mexican food."

"Yes, I know. In fact, everyone we know, knows." Seth said. Once Seth put their food on the table in front of Chloe, he sat down beside her. They said a quick prayer and begin to eat.

The man listened as Chloe and Seth sat quietly talking while they ate their food. He could see the struggle on Chloe's face as she tried not to cry. He knew of a flower shop close by so he stood up and hurried to buy one before the couple left. When he returned to the food court, there she sat. On seeing her he breathed a big sigh of relief. He then looked around and found a teenage boy and paid him five dollars to take the red rose to their table and hand it to Chloe.

"What? Who?" Chloe stammered, as the boy came up to the table and handed her the red rose. Her face turned pale. "It can't be! Seth, it can't be!" The boy stepped back embarrassed. He had thought he was doing a good thing and now he wasn't so sure.

While the man stood watching Chloe's reaction, her eyes began to fill with tears and she started searching the area in desperation. Seth stood up, helped Chloe to stand, grabbed the packages that were under the table and then they left the food court heading for their car.

The man was very pleased with her reaction. Wherever they had been, they were back. So now the game would begin again.

CHAPTER 1

After returning from another troubleshooting job for the company he worked for, Seth and Chloe walked hand in hand over to the table at the food court in the mall. Chloe sat down and with her right foot pushed her packages under the table. She watched Seth make his way directly to Casa Ole. The line wasn't very long so she knew it probably wouldn't take him very long. To pass the time Chloe's gaze started looking around the room. She waved at Seth as her eyes found his, but then continued on around the room traveling from table to table and then from face to face. Suddenly she stopped, her gaze collided with the man's at the next table. She felt the chills and the shivers begin going up and down her spine. Fear encompassed her very being. She looked for Seth and as his eyes met hers, she felt safe so she decided she had let her imagination get the best of her. Her eyes continued looking around the food court to keep herself occupied until Seth returned.

Their decision to return to the food court was a decision they had had a hard time making, but now here they were. Chloe had been keeping an eye on Seth ever since she had felt the chill and was grateful when he sat their food down on the table in front of her. They were both nervous for they both knew this was where the stalker had first decided Chloe was going to be his victim.

"Relax, Chloe. Let's just try and enjoy our meal. Okay?" Seth asked as he placed Chloe's taco salad in front of her. "We can get through this. If you decide it's too much, tell me and we'll go."

They sat eating quietly, but when Seth looked Chloe in the eyes, he could see they were full of unshed tears. After all this time, in the blink of an eye, her stalker, even though he was dead, had been able to steal the peace she had fought so hard to attain. Seth reached across the table placing his hand on top of hers hoping it would give her some comfort, but instead his action made the tears escape her eyes and begin to flow down her cheeks.

Chloe took Seth's hand and as she did, she began to squeeze it so tight that after a short time, Seth's fingers started going numb. Seth didn't say a word. He knew all she had been through, all that he had been through and now he just wanted her to know he was there for her. Slowly she began to release the pressure and it was only when she saw him wiggling his fingers, that she realized how hard she had been squeezing his hand.

"I am so sorry, Seth. I didn't realize... You should have said something."

"I know, Chloe. Believe me I would have said something before my fingers fell off." Seth said with a teasing grin.

Seth and Chloe continued to talk quietly not wanting to be overheard by anyone around them.

"You know, Seth, I look around at all these people as they sit talking and laughing. They don't have a care in the world and I remember the time when I didn't either. With all that we have been through over the last few months, I am surprised we both survived. But I guess if we can survive this, we can survive anything."

Chloe's eyes continued looking around at all the different people sitting in the food court.

Finally, she said, "You know, Seth, all the people sitting here are oblivious to the evil that could be sitting right beside them. I know I didn't have any idea someone was watching me. So I went about my merry little way not paying any attention to what was going on around me. What do you think made him pick me? Did I do something? Or not do something?"

"I don't know, Chloe. I guess we probably won't ever know. I wish I could tell you we won't ever have a problem again. But you know as well as I do, that just being in this world we are subject to the problems that come with it. Especially as Christians. Satan already has the non-believers so he roams around as a lion hunting for its prey waiting for a Christian to fall. And, bang, there it is. An opening. He does things just to get us to make the wrong choices. And, Chloe, we made it through because of love and commitment. Commitment to God and our commitment to each other. It may be hard and we may not always make the right choices, but we belong to Jesus so it's up to us to hold on to Him and to never let go."

"I know you're right, Seth, but sometimes it gets really hard. I've finished eating so whenever you're ready we can go."

"Give me a couple of minutes and I'll be ready, too."

While Chloe sat waiting for Seth to finish, once again she started looking around the food court. Her eyes glancing from here to there. One woman is having trouble getting her three kids to settle down and eat, while another one is sitting alone with a cup of coffee in her hand. Another man is sitting with his two sons talking softly to them as they listen intently. She wondered what he could be saying that held their attention so completely.

She continued looking around the food court and her gaze settled on a man standing off by himself just outside the food court area. He looked like the man that had been sitting beside her so she glanced at his table and he was gone. She continued looking around the room but her gaze kept returning to him. She was sure it was the man that had been sitting beside her and he was staring at her and he was holding something in his hand. She couldn't quite see what it was. So she looked away and continued to look around the room hoping he was probably doing the same thing she was doing. Maybe she was over reacting, but somehow she knew she wasn't.

Chloe continued looking around the room periodically, letting her gaze return to the area where the man was standing. He was always there and he was always staring at her.

"Seth, I'm sorry, but we really have to go."

"But I'm not through with my nachos."

"Seth, we need to go now. I'll explain when we get to the car."

"Okay! Okay! Can I at least take my nachos with me?"

Chloe glanced at the man one more time and as she did, he looked her straight in the eyes and gave her a big smile. Before she could get out of her chair a teenage boy approached their table.

"Is your name Chloe?"

"Yes, it is. Why?"

"A man paid me five dollars to give you this red rose and I just want to make sure you're the one I was supposed to give it to. He said you would understand."

Chloe looked at Seth as she said, "It can't be. Oh, Seth, it can't be."

Seth knew what the red rose meant as well as Chloe did and he immediately started looking around the room. Not seeing anyone who looked out of place Seth helped Chloe to stand, then bent over to pick up their packages. Once they were both standing, he steered Chloe in the direction of the door so they could return to their car.

"What's happening? Sean Delaney is dead. Surely there can't be another stalker?" Chloe questioned as they left the food court.

They both looked at each other not daring to voice the thoughts that were clamoring through their heads.

"Not again. Oh! please, Lord. Not again!"

CHAPTER 2

The man continued to watch Seth and Chloe. He didn't know why she hadn't picked up on the fact that she was being watched, but because she hadn't, he was able to watch her unrestricted. Chloe hadn't paid much attention at first, but now that he was staring straight at her, he saw the disbelief slowly make its way across her face. Though her gaze kept going around the room, it always came back to him. He had accomplished what he had set out to do. She was afraid and he wanted her to be afraid. He liked the power her fear gave him. He watched as they made their way out of the food court. His gaze never leaving Chloe until he spied his cousin's daughter, Andrea, approaching him with her shopping bags. He had wanted to take the game further, but he had forgotten about Andrea.

"Oh, well," the man sighed to himself. "There would be another day. She was back and that was all he needed to know."

Both Seth and Chloe began their drive home in complete silence. Since neither one knew what to say to the other, it was a long trip.

"Do you think we should stop by the Police Station and talk to Detective Bonner?" Seth asked, as they reached the outskirts of Livingston. "I know it may be a little soon, but it might be a good idea to touch base with him. Just in case. What do you think?"

"I don't know. I really don't know."

After entering town, Seth pulled into a parking lot, but was completely unaware of his surroundings. As was Chloe. If someone had asked either one of them later where they had parked, they would not have been able to tell them. Thirty minutes passed and still they sat in the parking lot unable to make up their minds as to what they should do.

Finally Seth said, "I know you think it's too soon, but I think we should at least talk to Detective Bonner. Something doesn't feel right and I know how upset you are. If we just talk to him, maybe, we can put all of this behind us, but we won't know until we talk to him. I didn't listen to you the first time and it almost got you killed. I am certainly not going to make that mistake again. We'll just give Detective Bonner the heads up. Okay?"

"I guess you're right. It just seems like it might be a little soon. I am also afraid I might have over reacted. But you're right let's go get Detective Bonner's perspective."

"If this was the very first time something like this had ever happened, Chloe," Seth said. "I would agree with you that going to talk to the detective was too soon, but it's not. It's better to be safe than sorry. Don't you agree?"

"Yes, I guess I do."

Seth and Chloe pulled out of the parking lot and headed toward the Police Station. Not sure they were doing the right thing, but wanting to make sure they were not doing the wrong thing, they pulled into the station and found an empty space and parked. Then walking hand in hand they headed toward the front door. When they reached it, Chloe stepped back allowing Seth to open the door for her. She had always appreciated Seth's chivalrousness and never more than now. It made her feel special, loved and safe.

Upon entering the room they asked the first person they met if they could talk to Detective Bonner. Pointing in the direction of the detective's desk they were told he had stepped out for a few minutes, but he should be back very soon. They could sit and wait for him or they could come back later. Since they were already there, they decided to sit and wait. They had been there several minutes and just as they decided they would talk to him later, Detective Bonner came striding toward his desk. Once he spotted them, he stopped talking to everyone and immediately headed in their direction.

"Seth, Chloe. How nice to see you. How can I help you today?"

"Right at this moment we're not sure."

Detective Bonner listened to Chloe as she relayed what had happened at the mall.

"To tell you the truth, Detective, we don't know what to make of the situation. We thought we were through with this whole thing and then out of the blue, it all seems to be starting over again. Seth and I stopped in some parking lot trying to decide whether to come see you or not. We're here so I guess you know what our decision was."

"We don't know what to do." Seth said. "If anything? Surely this can't be happening again?"

"I don't really know what to think." Detective Bonner said, as he looked at both Chloe and Seth noting how nervous they appeared to be. They were both sitting toward the front of their chairs with their hands tightly gripped in front of them. Chloe's legs were bouncing up and down so fast he didn't know how she did it without falling out of her seat.

"If you hadn't had this problem before, I would probably dismiss it, but all three of us know that is something we don't want to do. Chloe, your intuitiveness has proved right many times before. My gut tells me something else is going on, too. What, I don't know? I wish I did."

The detective looked at Chloe with a serious expression on his face. "It's too early for the police to get involved and I'm sorry about that, but that doesn't mean we are going to dismiss it either. I'm going to set up my own file and I would appreciate it if you would call and let me know if something doesn't feel right to you. We have to start somewhere."

"Thanks, Bob." Seth said. He and Chloe were never sure when to use their friend's first name or when to call him detective. "You can bet we'll be calling you. Probably more than you want to hear from us."

As Chloe walked out of earshot, Detective Bonner stopped Seth from walking away by touching him on the shoulder. "Seth, I want you to know I am taking this seriously. So please. Stay alert."

"Do you know something I don't know?"

"All I'm saying is pay attention to your surroundings. From experience, I know Chloe is very intuitive so until we know for sure whether something is going on or not. Stay alert!!! And tell her to do the same."

"Thanks, for the heads up." Seth told the detective.

"What was Detective Bonner saying to you when he stopped you from leaving with me?" Chloe asked her husband while he was in the process of opening the door for her.

"He was telling me, us, to stay alert. Stay alert and be aware of our surroundings until we know for sure what is going on and whether or not we have something to worry about?"

CHAPTER 3

The man was right. They stopped at the police station on their way home. He had to hurry to get Andrea home and then get to the police station before they got there. He actually accomplished it. Now he watched as they got out of their car, with Seth getting out first. Then he went to Chloe's side opening the door for her. Once they were both out of the car, they grasped each other's hand as if it was a life line and walked toward the front door of the police station.

He sat there for quite a long time waiting for Seth and Chloe to return. When they did, they got in their car and just sat there for several minutes completely still. At first he wondered what they were doing and why they didn't just start the car and leave, but he had been part of the stalking off and on from the beginning and he just knew they were praying.

"Let them say their prayers," he thought to himself. "It would make no difference in the end." He had watched as plan after plan had gone awry, but sometimes things just happened that way, and it didn't have a thing to do with praying. At least he didn't think so.

Murder by proxy. What a concept? At times he had watched what John Bledsoe and Sean Delaney were doing, but he had kept his distance. Letting things play out as they would. He had enjoyed watching it all taking place, but it was time to bring things to a close. He was tired. He wanted to move on. He just couldn't open another door until the present one was closed.

―――――

As Seth and Chloe sat in front of the police station, they bowed their heads and began to pray.

"Heavenly Father," Seth said quietly. "We don't know what lies ahead of us, but we know that You do and for that we are truly thankful. In Proverbs 3:5, You tell us to trust in You and lean not to our own understanding. So, Father, that is exactly what we are going to do. Trust and lean. We leave this matter in Your hands and we ask it in the Name of Your Son, Jesus. Amen."

―――――

The man smiled to himself as he tried to listen. The windows were down, but all he was able to hear was the "Amen". He got out of his car and strode toward the doors of the police station wanting them to think he had business there, but once they had backed up and began to drive out of the parking lot, he changed his direction and returned to his car. He didn't have to hurry to follow them because he already knew where they were going.

―――――

"What are we going to do, Seth? I am afraid it is starting all over and I don't know if I can make it this time." Chloe said, as she and Seth were headed home.

"I don't know what we're going to do, but I do know God is going to be with us while we're going through it. We just chose to trust and lean. We made that choice, Chloe, and now. Well, now we are going to have to follow through with that choice." Seth reiterated once more.

"Am I apprehensive? Yes, I am. Is my mind running ninety miles a minute in all directions? Yes, it is. But, Chloe, I know the only way we are going to survive this is to take one day at a time and to leave each day in God's hands. I know non-Christians think we use God as a crutch and maybe we do. But at the same time they have their own crutches, such as, drinking too much, doing drugs and choosing to be workaholics. There are so many things that are out there that other people choose to use. I would so much rather choose to be in God's hands. Wouldn't you?"

"I know you're right. I guess I'm just tired."

"Trust and lean, Chloe. Take one day at a time," and with that statement, they both slipped into silence.

———

Somehow the man caught up with them. For a while, he followed them from a safe distance. He was close enough to keep an eye on them, but far enough away so Seth would not become suspicious.

It was almost time for them to turn off the highway onto the dirt road that led to their house. He sped up and passed them leaving them behind. He wanted to get to their house before they did, but he didn't have much time. He reached the side road. It was a small trail that eventually ended up at an oil rig that had been placed there years before. So he turned, and when he reached the area behind their house, he parked deep in the bushes. He got out and went and stood by a big tree located not far from the back patio of their house. Then he crouched down and he waited.

———

The closer Chloe and Seth got to their turnoff the slower Seth drove. He passed the first turnoff because neither one of them was mentally ready to face what might be coming their way. The second turnoff appeared and once again Seth drove right past it. When the third turnoff appeared, he knew this was it. So he made a left hand turn, turning onto the dirt road that would take them back to their house. He was having to back track, but neither one of them seemed to mind.

When they finally arrived at the driveway to their house, they pulled up in front of the mailbox and picked up their mail. They could put it off no longer. Seth drove as slow as he possibly could up the driveway. It was a long driveway because he had to drive through the pasture to get to the house. He then pulled up to the garage doors, pushed the opener, but did not pull into the garage.

"You know, Seth. It doesn't matter what is going on around you there is no place like home."

"I agree. Come on. Let's go in." Seth said, pulling into the garage and shutting the garage door behind him.

———

The man crouched down beside the big tree in the woods behind the Kelley's house. As it turned out, he had had more time to settle in than he had thought he would have, but now he was settled in and they were home.

———

Chloe went to the patio door and stood looking out toward the woods. She stood there several minutes remembering all that had taken place. Finally Seth called her, so she pulled the curtains shut and retreated back into the house.

When she closed the curtains, the man smiled to himself. She used to leave her curtains open all the time, but that was before John Bledsoe and Sean Delaney. What a disaster that had turned out to be. He sat staring at the house, but since it was beginning to get dark and he couldn't see anything anyway, he decided to leave and return the next day.

Chloe finally sat down beside Seth thinking she might want to watch a little television before going to bed. Darkness filled the room along with the tension of the day. Chloe was comfortable being in Seth's arms as she slowly drifted off to sleep.

Seth could tell by the heaviness of Chloe's body when she finally went to sleep. Instead of waking her up to go to bed, he just shifted a little and settled into the comfort of the chair. As he lay there, his memory kept going over the events of when he almost lost her.

Late into the night Seth continued to pray until exhaustion finally overcame him and he drifted off to sleep with his last thought being just a simple plea of, "Oh, God. Help us."

CHAPTER 4

The man was already in place when the sun came up the
next morning. He stood by his favorite tree smiling to
himself as he watched the back of the house. He had
come up with the most brilliant plan last night, or so he thought,
and he could not wait to put it into action.

He had stopped in one of the retail stores that stayed open all
night and picked up some red roses. He had also picked up a vase
and some bottled water. Now that he had what he needed, he
stood in the woods behind their house.

Since coming up with his plan, he was in such a good humor
that he had smiled and said hi to everyone he met and they did
the same. Not one of those people knew the reason behind his
good humor or the reason he bought the red roses. He was sure
they would not approve of his actions. There was one young girl
that tried to flirt with him and if he hadn't been on a mission, he
might have stopped and talked to her.

While it was still dark, he made his way to the Kelley's house.
He approached from the side so he didn't have to fight all the
trees and the brush. He took one red rose from the bunch of
roses that were laying on the seat beside him and placed it in the
vase. After making his way to the patio, he put the red rose on
the patio table hoping Chloe would be the first to see it.

He was already back in place when he saw the light come on in the kitchen. Chloe was standing in front of the kitchen window. It was a large window placed in front of the sink. After watching for a moment, he decided she was making coffee like she did every morning. Once again it amazed him how many people did not shut their curtains at night. She had shut the patio door curtains, but had left the curtains over the sink wide open.

He continued to watch as she got herself a cup of coffee. Then for a moment he couldn't see her. While he waited for her to return to his sight, he hoped she would not sit in the house, but would come out and sit on the patio. He waited, but she didn't come outside.

Then there she was. She pulled back the patio curtains and was standing in the doorway. She continued walking toward the patio table and was in the progress of sitting her coffee cup down when she saw the red rose.

As she made her way to the patio table, she looked up trying to find the woodpecker that was making all the noise. She continued to walk toward the table and as she went to set her coffee on the table, she saw the red rose.

When Chloe saw the red rose, her heart seemed to stop beating. Fear overcame her. She avoided the rose as her eyes stared off into the woods.

"Seth," Chloe yelled as she stood looking at the rose. "Seth," this time Chloe's yell was more of a plea as she slowly sat down on the patio chair.

Seth came running out of the house. "Chloe, are you alright? What are you yelling about?"

"Why didn't you come when I first called you?"

"I guess I was in the bathroom and didn't hear you." Seth's eyes followed the direction in which Chloe was looking and that was when he saw the red rose.

"Where did the rose come from?"

"If you didn't put it there, and I don't think you did. I guess we probably know who did. Are you thinking what I'm thinking?" Chloe said, looking at Seth with eyes full of tears.

"Yes, I guess I am."

He almost laughed out loud as he watched their reaction. Seth he didn't really care about, but her reaction was more than he could ever have hoped for. The dread on Seth's face was an extra bonus. Everything was falling into place. He was ready for the game to begin.

CHAPTER 5

"May we speak to Detective Bonner, please?"

Seth and Chloe went back into the house, got dressed, and drove immediately into town. They weren't one hundred percent sure, but they were ninety-nine percent sure the stalking was beginning again.

"If you can wait for just a minute, I'll check and see," one of the other detectives answered them.

The detective turned and asked if anyone had seen Detective Bonner. After seeing Chloe was in the room, Detective Roberts came over and told them he had just stepped out for a minute and would be right back.

"Seth, Chloe, what can I do for the two of you?" Detective Bonner asked. "I sure hope the reason you're here isn't the one I think it is," he said reaching his hand in Seth's direction.

"As much as I wish we could say we're here for something else, we're not. We are pretty sure we have a problem." Seth said, as he told the detective what had just happened that morning.

Chloe only interrupted so she could tell the part when Seth had not arrived yet.

"Come on in and let's sit down and see if we can figure out

what to do?"

"Before we get started I would like to know one thing," Seth said, as the three of them sat down at Detective Bonner's desk.

"What's that, Seth?"

"Have you ever heard of being stalked three times? I realize the first two stalkers were paid by someone else. Now whether this third one was the instigator or not we don't know. Bledsoe and Delaney are dead. Is there a connection here that I am completely missing?"

"No, Seth, I personally have never heard of that happening. Doesn't mean it hasn't. I just haven't heard of it."

"So what do we do now, Bob? Is this going to start all over again? It's unnerving to think something is going to happen and we don't even know what it is. We don't even know who is going to do it."

"I really don't know what to tell you, Seth. At this point we don't have anything to go on. I do stress the ANYTHING part. I will write up what you have told me and put it in your folder, and place a high priority beside your name, but at this point, other than checking the known stalkers in this area, our hands are tied because, as of this moment in time, nothing has taken place," Detective Bonner cautioned.

"Now, the red rose. That is a substantial clue. We think something is going to happen. But, what? Neither you nor I know what? The only thing I can stress at this point is to stay vigilant. Be aware of your surroundings. And, Chloe, you need to pay attention to your intuition. It has served you well in the past so use it and most of all listen to it."

Seth and Chloe left the police station in a cloud of gloom. As they got in the car, Seth turned to Chloe and said, "Let's go out and eat. I am sure you don't want to fix anything when we get home and you know I don't. So, where would you like to go?"

"I don't know, Seth. Anywhere you pick is fine with me. I'm hungry, but I'm not sure I feel like eating right now."

"Okay, let's go to the S&S Cafe?"

"Sounds good to me."

Even though the cafe wasn't that far from the police station, they decided to drive over and park behind it. Any other time they would have walked because it was so close, but today they just couldn't muster up the strength or the want to. So they drove.

The man was sitting in his car watching and waiting for them to come out of the station. He decided he would follow them if the situation arose, but since he knew where they lived, he wasn't all that concerned about it. Doing what he was doing was just part of the plan and he enjoyed it.

He pulled into the parking space right beside them. They were still in their car talking and didn't pay any attention to him. As he watched from his car, they both got out of their car, with Seth opening the door for Chloe like he always did. They headed toward the S&S Cafe hand in hand.

He didn't want to be too far behind them on entering the restaurant because he was hoping he would be able to sit close to Chloe. Not too close, though, because he was afraid she might remember his face from the mall.

The man got out of his car and when he stood up, he was able to see Chloe's side of the car. He had been ready to hurry after them, but he had an idea. He stopped, took a few steps backward, opened his car door once again, picked up the tool for unlocking car doors, and at the same time picked up a red rose that he had sitting in a vase on the floor of the car.

He opened Chloe's car door putting the red rose on her seat. He then covered it with a page of the newspaper he had laying on the front seat of his car. His job was completed. He started walking in the direction of the cafe once again. He was smiling and didn't care whether he sat beside Chloe or not, but it would be a big bonus if he was able to pull it off.

He had been smiling a lot the last couple of days. Everything seemed to be falling into place and he was glad he'd decided to keep some red roses in the car at all times, so if the situation presented itself, he would have one handy.

When he walked into the cafe, he seated himself across the room from the Kelley's. He would have liked to have been closer, but they were really busy so he took what he could get. He watched and enjoyed as Chloe interacted with her husband while they were eating. He was in no hurry, so he flirted with one of the girls sitting close to him. When he finished, he decided it was time to leave. He paid his bill and returned to his car. He pulled out of his parking space, but he only went down the street a short distance before he found another one and parked once again.

He pulled out his binoculars so he could check and make sure he could see them thru the lens before he shut the motor off. As he sat in his car waiting for the Kelley's to come out of the cafe, he watched a young couple, a single man, and a family of four all come out before they did.

Finally Chloe and Seth came out. Chloe was laughing so hard she could hardly catch her breath. Seth was staring at his wife thoroughly enjoying her laughter. It had been a long time since he had seen her laugh with such abandonment. It seemed as if the cloud that hung over them, had for the moment disappeared. Seth walked ahead of Chloe so he could open the door for her. But, once the door was open and Chloe was in the process of sitting down, she saw the newspaper. She reached down to move it out of her way and that's when she saw the red rose.

"Seth!" Chloe cried, staring at the red rose.

Seeing the red rose, Seth immediately began searching the vicinity for anyone who seemed out of place. Forgetting that he had been helping Chloe to get in the car.

"I'm sorry, Chloe." Seth said, trying to keep his wife from falling. Between Seth's attention being drawn elsewhere and Chloe trying to preserve whatever she could for Detective Bonner, they both began to lose their balance.

The man almost laughed out loud as he watched when Chloe found the red rose. He knew she knew immediately where it had come from and tried to stop the momentum of her body. She failed. When she fell to the side of the car, she caused Seth to lose his balance. They were both in the process of landing on the pavement when a young man held out his hand. "Would you two like some help?"

CHAPTER 6

C hloe and Seth started walking toward the police station again. Every few steps one or the other would turn around to check their car. They didn't want anything to happen to the evidence, but at the same time Seth knew Chloe did not and could not stay there.

As they approached the station, Detective Roberts was coming out the front door. "Weren't you two just here?"

"Yes, we were, but a situation has come up and we really need to talk to Detective Bonner."

"I'm pretty sure he just stepped out for a sandwich. In fact, I think he went to the "Watering Hole". You know, the restaurant across from the courthouse. He did tell me to let him know anytime you called. Although, I doubt very seriously if he thought it would be this soon. Hold on just a minute. Let me check." Detective Roberts pulled his cell phone out of his pocket and called the detective.

"He is there and he said for you two to come on over and you could talk there. That is if you want to?"

Detective Roberts, Seth and Chloe decided to walk to the "Watering Hole" because it was so close. As the trio passed in front of the restaurant's window, they could see the detective quietly watching them. He continued to watch them from the moment they entered through the door until they walked up to his table. When they reached his table, he stood up and with a welcoming gesture indicated they should all sit down with him.

"If you don't need me, Bob?" Detective Roberts said. "I think I'll go catch up on some paperwork, but if I can help in any way, I'll be glad to stay."

"Kyle, I think it would be better if you sit in on this conversation. I'm not sure where it's going, but you have been in on it almost from the beginning."

"Okay, if you think I can help?" Detective Roberts said, as he sat down at the table with everyone else.

"Would you like some coffee, Detective?"

" I don't think so. At least not right now."

"How about you, Chloe? Would you like some?"

"I don't think so, Seth."

The waitress approached their table. Seth looked at her and told her he would have some coffee, but no one else wanted any.

"Okay," Detective Bonner began, as he started the conversation, while looking directly at Seth and Chloe. "Who is going to tell me what is going on?"

"I'll start and then Chloe can tell her part when I finish. It's only been a couple of hours since we talked to you. I guess I'll start there."

After Seth relayed his part of the story, Chloe started with her seeing the newspaper, moving it with her left hand and then seeing the red rose lying underneath.

Seth closed with him immediately looking around for anyone that might be looking at them. He could find no one.

"First of all, whoever did this was probably already gone. Second, did you happen to leave your car doors unlocked? Third, was the newspaper yours or do you think it belonged to the stalker?" Detective Bonner asked as he looked directly at Seth and Chloe.

"No," Chloe said. "The car was clean. We didn't leave a newspaper in it, but even if we had, how would it get in my seat with a red rose underneath? It makes no sense."

"Kyle, if you could get forensics to go over the car, I would appreciate it. Especially the newspaper. Usually there is nothing for us to find, but he could have made a mistake this time."

"Sure, I'll see you back at the station." The trio solemnly watched Detective Roberts make his departure.

"Seth, Chloe, I know this is going to be hard for you to understand, but until we see if anything shows up on the car or the newspaper, we still don't have any evidence to act upon. Hopefully, he will slip up soon, and the sooner the better." Detective Bonner stopped then started again.

"I don't like to say this either because I don't want to scare you any more than you already are, but this guy, whoever he might be, has done his homework. He knows where you live and for whatever reason you have appeared on his radar screen and stayed there. I know......."

"Bob," Seth said interrupting the detective as he was speaking. "Is this in any way connected to the two other stalkings? It's really hard to believe that three men have decided to stalk my wife."

"We are working on that premise at the moment, but right now we still don't have anything concrete to go on. If anything else happens, let me know immediately. And don't touch anything. You never know what he may slip up on. I am sorry I wish I could do more."

Detective Bonner left the restaurant wishing that he had more to go on so he could help the Kelley's. There just wasn't anything he could do. Yet!

"Seth, do you think he's watching us right now?" Chloe said, as she watched the detective until she lost sight of him.

Since neither one had ordered anything to eat, and Seth had already finished his coffee, they decided they would rent a car and go home. Then they would wait for the police to call them to let them know they were through with their car and they could pick it up. Their car was completely clean so they knew it shouldn't take long.

As they waited for the rental car in front of the restaurant, Chloe looked at Seth. "I love you, Seth. No matter how this turns out I want you to know I love you. We both know that sometimes God's plan for us is not exactly what we want, but He always works on our behalf for the good."

"I love you, too, Chloe, and we will get through this. Trust and lean. Remember?"

"I remember."

CHAPTER 7

The man had accomplished what he had set out to do. Chloe was afraid. Seth was afraid for her. He watched as Seth, Chloe and Detective Roberts approached the Watering Hole Restaurant. Detective Bonner was sitting in the little alcove at the front of the restaurant which was located right in front of a big picture window.

He continued to watch as the trio entered through the front door going straight to Detective Bonner's table. They all sat down and started talking. He couldn't hear what was being said so he decided to leave. Besides he wanted to go to his brother's house and see if he could borrow his motorcycle.

He was in no hurry to get to Chloe's house. His brother hadn't been too happy to see him, but he finally convinced him he would bring it back before he had to go to work the next morning.

He needed the motorcycle because it was so much harder to locate and so much easier to hide than a car. He knew at some point the police would start searching the woods behind Chloe's house. Probably not right now, but he wanted to be able to leave quickly just in case they decided today was the day. He hid it behind a tree, close to the road, in some brush.

The man was standing against the tree when he heard a car coming up the drive. When he heard the garage door open, he knew for sure that the Kelley's were home. He stayed where he was and just watched and waited.

He had enjoyed today immensely. In fact, he could not have asked for a better day. He was able to play the game twice. Although, he had no doubt that Seth and Chloe had not enjoyed it nearly as much as he had.

He watched the house until the sun went down. He would periodically see one or the other as they moved about the house, but no one came outside. Finally, the light in the bedroom came on and all the other lights went off. He assumed they were in for the night so he moved quietly back to where he hid the motorcycle and drove away.

Seth and Chloe were getting ready for bed when Chloe said, "Seth, I'm scared. It's starting all over again. What does this person want? Why did he pick me? What did the other two men have to do with what is going on now? So many questions, but no answers."

"I know. I know. We may have to trust and lean a lot more than we thought in the beginning, but we made a choice."

Chloe sat down beside Seth. He took her hands in his and once again began to pray, "Father, we are in trouble. Big trouble. We ask You to prepare us for the days ahead. Deliver us from the evil that has once again set its eyes on Chloe. In Jesus' Name we pray. Amen."

Chloe stood up and went around to her side of the bed. She sat down then reached over to shut her bedside lamp off. Once the light was off, she moved to snuggle under the covers. Seth did the same and then they both moved toward the center. As they both lay in each other's arms, they drifted off to sleep.

As the morning sun came through their bedroom window, Chloe laid very still so she would not wake Seth. She didn't know when, but at some point during the night she had decided it might be a good idea to take a self-defense class. She knew beyond a shadow of a doubt if Seth was around, he would protect her with his life. She also knew Seth could not be with her twenty-four seven.

She was so convinced she was right that she got up and went to their computer and logged on to find the nearest self-defense class. There was one listed in Livingston and one in Woodville. Since they were both close to their house, she decided she would check out the one in Woodville after Seth went to work. She printed out the address and since she was already up, decided to put on some coffee and fix Seth some breakfast. Today was Seth's first day back at work since they had returned from his troubleshooting job in Venezuela. He usually stopped and picked him up something to eat along the way so this would be a surprise for him.

"Wow!" Seth exclaimed, walking into the kitchen. "To what do I owe this honor?"

"Funny. I was up already and decided to surprise you," Chloe said, as she poured Seth a cup of coffee.

"Bacon, eggs, toast, coffee. What's going on, Chloe?"

"I don't want you to get spoiled."

"Why not? I like being spoiled every once in awhile." Seth joked and began to eat his breakfast. "This is great. What are you going to do today?"

"I thought I would check out a self-defense class I found online. There are two. One in Livingston and one in Woodville. Neither one is that far. But I thought today I would check out the one in Woodville. Once the place opens up, I'll go in and see what I can find out."

"You know, Chloe, I think that is a really good idea. Let me know what you find out." Seth finished his cup of coffee, got all of his stuff together and kissed Chloe goodbye. He was all ready to go when he decided it might be better if Chloe took her daily shower now while he was still at home.

"Chloe, it would really make me feel better if you would take a quick shower now while I'm here. I forgot I needed to make a couple of phone calls. So if you will do it now while I am making the calls, I would appreciate it."

"That's a good idea."

Chloe hadn't liked the idea of taking a shower after Seth left, but she wasn't going to say anything. There was just something unnerving about being closed off in the bathroom away from the rest of the house, and once finished, the struggle of having to make your way to the front not knowing if someone had been able to gain entrance while you were in the back showering.

She hadn't always felt like that, but awhile back she and Seth had watched an old movie called 'Psycho.' Combined with that movie and her stalker she was always peeking out from behind the shower curtain to make sure someone had not come in while she had the curtain closed.

With this new threat, Chloe wasn't sure she would even have taken a shower once Seth had left. She didn't know if the phone calls were real or not. It was just like Seth to tell her that so she wouldn't feel guilty. Real or not she was thankful.

"Seth, I'm out!" Chloe yelled as she finished toweling off and entered the bedroom. "If you give me a second, I'll put on some clothes and you can go. Seth, do you hear me? Where are you?" Just as she was ready to call again, Seth came in from the patio. "Seth, you scared me when you didn't answer." Chloe said, as she punched him on the arm.

"I'm sorry. I guess I wasn't thinking. I decided to water the plants on the patio while I was waiting for you to take your shower."

"I thought you said you had a couple of phone calls to make."

"I guess you caught me. I didn't want you to be alone in the house while you were taking a shower. I watched 'Psycho', too, remember."

"Thanks, Seth. I appreciate it, but you better leave or you're going to be late for work."

"I know. I know. You've got to promise me, Chloe, that you will be careful and stay aware of your surroundings at all times. Okay?"

"I will. I promise." Chloe said, as she kissed Seth one more time before he left for work.

Seth picked up his briefcase and his computer and headed for the door located between the house and the garage. After getting into his car, he pressed the garage door opener and waved to Chloe at the same time. When he exited the garage, he again pushed the button so the garage door would close behind him.

Chloe returned to the bedroom and finished dressing. It was still too early to go to town so she poured herself another cup of coffee and went out to sit on the patio.

It was so nice and so peaceful. She had always loved sitting out here all alone, snuggled into her nice warm blanket. This time alone had always belonged to her and God. As she talked to Him, she could feel His presence. Others may think she was crazy, but let them think what they will. She didn't care.

————

He watched while she sat there not moving a muscle. He had watched her too many times before to not know what she was doing now. She was praying. He wondered if she ever got tired of it. He also wondered if she really believed that it helped her.

He didn't think it did. Everything was going his way. He enjoyed the feeling of power her fear gave him. He knew at some time she was going to be his. He could feel it in his bones and it felt good.

CHAPTER 8

The man didn't know why Chloe hadn't picked up on his presence this morning, but she hadn't. He stood silent and still and just watched her. He enjoyed this time of the morning although his reasons he knew were very different from hers.

Last night he had returned his brother's motorcycle. He knew he couldn't borrow it too often, otherwise his brother might not let him borrow it at all. And there were times when it was exactly what he needed.

He noticed Chloe was dressed and decided she might be going to town. He really wanted to follow her today to see what she was up to. So when she got up and took her plate into the kitchen, he knew she was getting close to being ready to walk out the door. When she shut and locked the patio door, he backed up and ran the short distance to his car. He climbed in behind the steering wheel and drove toward the main dirt road. He wanted to see which direction she would take without being too obvious that he was watching her.

He waited, but she didn't come. He decided she must have gone the other direction. He drove out onto the road and turned in the direction of her house, but he wasn't able to tell if she had left yet or not.

Just as he looked toward the house, he noticed she was pulling out of the garage. His timing was perfect. He did a swift u-turn and returned to the dirt road. He drove far enough back so she wouldn't be able to see him, but close enough to see whether she passed in front of him or not.

Chloe drove right in front of him. He waited a few seconds and then pulled onto the road right behind her. He knew when she reached the highway, she could lose him very easily. But he knew, if he lost her, it wasn't a big problem. Since he knew where she lived, it wasn't as important that he knew where she was going. When she returned later, he would be there. Everything seemed to be going his way and he wanted to keep it that way.

Once Chloe had searched the internet and found there was a self-defense class in Woodville, she could hardly contain her excitement. She was actively doing something so as not to become a victim.

As she entered town, she followed the directions she had found on the internet and pulled up in front of the Tae-Kwan-Do building. She got there before the first class was to begin so she was able to talk to the owner. After talking to him, she knew this was something she could do and it would be to her benefit to do it. She hated this feeling of helplessness. She signed up for the class and found out that she could start the next day.

Chloe was filled with relief. With this small action, she no longer felt like a victim. She felt empowered. She had just taken her life back or so she thought. She decided that since she was already in town, she would do her shopping before going home.

She drove to Walmart and began to meander through the store enjoying her new found freedom, but then it was time to go. She walked to the front of the store and got in the check-out lane.

After placing her groceries on the conveyor belt, Chloe glanced up and saw a man watching her from the doorway. She looked away so she could put the rest of her items on the conveyer belt. When she finally completed her task and got up the nerve to check and see if he was still there, she found that he was.

The cashier got her attention by telling her the amount she owed. Chloe again looked away so she could pay her bill. Once she had completed her purchase, she headed toward the door where he was still standing and when she passed him, he smiled at her. Her legs got weak so she decided to sit down on the bench in the foyer and just as she did, he started talking to some other women. They were laughing and carrying on and having a good time. She decided she was just being paranoid. She looked at him one more time as he left through the front door of the store. The women he had been talking to reentered the store while he made his way to his car.

Chloe didn't know what she was going to do. The words Detective Bonner had emphasized the last time they had seen him were, "Be aware of your surroundings at all times. And to rely on her intuition." She had felt threatened when that man had smiled at her, but was she overreacting because of her situation. She didn't know.

She decided she had been sitting there long enough so she got up and started walking toward her car. Now she was paying attention to everyone that was even close to her. She got in the car, put her seatbelt on, and headed for home.

Chloe started to call Seth and tell him what had happened. Since she wasn't sure herself, she decided not to. She also didn't want to worry him, but she was definitely glad she had signed up for the self-defense class.

———

The man passed Chloe just as they were both leaving town. Not wanting to call attention to himself, he pulled in front of her and went on down the highway. He needed to get back to 'the tree' before she got home.

CHAPTER 9

Detective Bonner was really stumped. He and Detective Roberts had been tossing the elements of this case back and forth all morning and still could not come up with anything concrete that they could look into other than what they had already done.

"You know, Bob. I don't know what else we can do until this guy makes a mistake. He seems to know exactly what he is doing. He knows the Kelley's routine down to a T. At least as much as anyone can."

"I know and I'm really concerned about Mrs. Kelley since we both know she's the target. At the same time, if Mr. Kelley gets in his way, I don't think this man would hesitate one second in killing him."

"Let's go get some lunch over at the S&S Cafe. I'm hungry and I need a break. How about you?" Detective Roberts asked. "We really need a break in this case. It is hard to believe we have nothing to go on. Nothing!"

———

Chloe pulled into their garage closing the garage doors behind her. On entering the house she put her keys on the table then returned to the garage to get the groceries. She kept thinking she should call Seth and tell him about the incident at the store. When she finished putting everything up and the kitchen was clean again, she picked up her cell phone. He needed to be aware of what was going on.

Chloe had another thought. It might be a good idea to start keeping track of those incidents where she felt threatened. They may be nothing, but her tracking may help. She decided to go out on the patio while she talked to Seth. Just as she sat down, her cell phone rang. It was Seth.

"Hi Seth, I was just going to call you. Do you have time to talk for a minute or is this one of those checking to see if you're alright calls?"

"Funny, Chloe. But it is one of those we can talk for a minute calls. I wanted to find out how your excursion went this morning."

"That's what I wanted to talk to you about. I have two things I wanted to tell you."

"Okay. Shoot. What's on your mind?"

"First, I stopped at the Tae-Kwan-Do place and talked to them about self-defense classes. It sounded good so I signed up. I start tomorrow. I really am looking forward to it."

"Did you pick up some information for me?"

"Sure did. I picked up what they had and then decided to go shopping." Remembering what had happened at Wal-Mart made her throat start to close up and tears threatened to fall.

Seth heard the change in her voice and asked, "What happened, Chloe?"

"I know it's probably going to sound silly, but at the time it really bothered me." Chloe told Seth all about what had happened at Wal-Mart.

As Seth listened, his concern for Chloe grew. "I'm glad you signed up for those classes. If we hadn't been through all of this before, we might be tempted to slough it off, but now we know better. Everything is important. Continue to be aware of your surroundings at all times just like Detective Bonner said."

"I know. I know."

"I'm serious, Chloe. My own little addendum would be "keep God in the loop." You know what that means?"

"Yes, I know what that means. It seems as if I am praying non-stop and getting nowhere."

"You know that's not true, Chloe. And I am praying non-stop, too."

"Second, when I came out to call you, I had another idea. It might be helpful if when I feel threatened at any time no matter where I am, I should write it down. Keeping track of the day, time, where, and what happened. What do you think?"

"I think it's a good idea, Chloe. It might be the one thing that could break this case. You never know."

Chloe could hear the phone ringing in Seth's office. "I guess our talk time is over. I love you. Have a good day. Bye." she said, as she quickly hung up.

Chloe sat quietly enjoying her surrounding after she hung up from talking to Seth. In her mind she once again played over the events of the day. All of a sudden, from out of nowhere, she felt like she was being watched. Her first thought was, "Oh, God. No. Not again. I am really getting tired of this."

She had had this feeling so many times before she knew exactly what it was. Once again this person, this man, had taken away her peace. She had wanted to sit outside, but that was no longer possible. She sat there for a moment trying to get her thoughts together. She didn't want him to know she knew he was out there.

After a moment, she got up and went into the house taking all of her stuff with her. It was all she could do to keep the tears from falling, and when she shut the patio door behind her, she locked it then pulled the curtains shut.

The man watched her as she closed the patio door. But when she locked it and pulled the curtains shut, he knew he had accomplished his plan for the day. FEAR.

Detective Bonner returned to his desk. He had other cases he needed to be working on, but this one really bothered him. Not only were the Kelley's friends, but this case seemed to have no end. Chloe had had a stalker twice before and now it seemed as if there was going to be a third. What was going on here?

The Kelley's and the Bonners had become friends during Chloe's last two stalkers. They had seen a lot of each other. First, in the office and then they had started coming to their house for hamburgers. Julie Bonner and Chloe had hit it off and had become fast friends.

As he sat there deep in thought, his mind returned to the final moments of Chloe's previous case. The day they had finally caught Chloe's stalker, Sean Delaney. Could he have missed something? What could it have been? Sean Delaney was dead. It should have ended then and there. So what was going on now? The detective leaned back in his chair balancing it on its back two legs as the back hit the wall. His fingers were interlocked and his hands rested on the back of his head. Everyone around him knew this was his favorite position when he was thinking. They also knew not to bother him. Especially if his eyes were closed. And closed they were.

A memory flitted across his mind. He couldn't believe he had forgotten it. Not that it would help much, but still.

Chloe's old file was sitting on his desk just under the new one he had started the first day they had come in. He reached for the file and went through it page by page. When he got to the last page of his work report, he had put a p.s. after he had signed his name.

Now he remembered. He went over it in his head as if it were a motion picture. The coroner had pronounced Sean Delaney dead. The paramedics had made sure Chloe was okay and were getting ready to leave. He was going to take Chloe to the hospital to see her husband.

As he stood by his car door, he had had the strangest feeling. The hairs on the back of his neck had stood straight up. His eyes had traveled in a complete circle as they checked the darkness of the woods surrounding them.

He had ignored it at the time, but now, now he wished he had paid more attention to that feeling. He had been so happy that this case was solved that over time the remembrance of that feeling had slowly left his mind.

"Julie," Detective Bonner said as he picked up the phone and called his wife.

"Hi, sweetheart. What's up?"

"I was just thinking it might be nice to have Seth and Chloe over for hamburgers. We haven't really had them over for awhile and I know they are back from Venezuela. How about tonight?"

"Tonight. Bob, do you realize what time it is?" Julie said, as she looked at the clock.

"Oops! Sorry, Julie, I actually had not even looked at the time. I guess it is a little late. How about tomorrow night? I'll cook hamburgers out on the grill. All you have to do is come up with all that other stuff."

"I would love to invite Seth and Chloe over, but something tells me you have an ulterior motive. Am I right? What's really going on?"

"I'll explain what I can when I get home tonight. Right now I would appreciate it if you would call Chloe and make arrangements for them to come over."

"Will do. Any special time?"

"Sixish would probably be a good time. Is that a good time for you? We can make it later if you want too?"

"Bob, you do realize it is time for you to come home. Right?"

"I do now. Why don't you call Chloe and I'll finish up here and head for home. Love, ya. Bye."

Julie hung up the phone and immediately called Chloe. "Chloe, this is Julie."

"Julie, it's great to hear from you."

"It has been awhile hasn't it? Bob just told me you and Seth were back. So I thought I would call and see if you would like to come over for hamburgers tomorrow night. It has been awhile and I would love to see you. You can tell me all about your adventures in Venezuela."

"You're right. It has been awhile and we would love to come over. I'll check with Seth later, but I am sure it will be alright. What time?"

"Sixish. If that's alright with you?"

"Sounds fine to me. I'm looking forward to getting together. It's been awhile and I've missed you. Is there something I can bring?"

"No, just yourselves."

"Thanks, Julie. We'll see you tomorrow night."

CHAPTER 10

Seth and Chloe pulled up in front of the Bonner's house. Since Julie had called yesterday, Chloe had been looking forward to tonight. She had the feeling Bob had an ulterior motive, but she didn't care. It had been awhile since she and Julie had been able to get together and she had every intention of enjoying herself.

Seth was feeling the same way. It would be nice to sit and visit and not have to worry about Chloe's stalker. How much safer could you get than a detective's house?

They got out of the car just as Detective Bonner came around the side of the house. He walked through the little gate that was bordered on each side by a hedge and as he did, he called to them.

"Seth, Chloe. Glad you could make it," he said giving Chloe a hug and Seth a hearty hand shake.

"It's been awhile," Detective Bonner said, as he led them through the gate to the patio in the backyard.

"I just got home so we are running a little behind," he continued. "Julie has everything ready so I can start cooking as soon as we get hungry."

"I think we all know something else is going on here. So let's talk about it and get it over with then we can enjoy ourselves. How does that sound?" Seth asked. Everyone agreed so they all sat down.

"First of all, Chloe, I have to apologize to you and tell you how sorry I am."

"What does that mean, Bob? I don't understand."

"It means I remembered something I had forgotten and something I should have followed through on." He then proceeded to tell Chloe and Seth what he had remembered at the end of the Sean Delaney episode. "But, we had just closed the case and it got lost in the shuffle. My apologies," and with a regret he didn't usually feel, the detective continued.

"Earlier this evening I sent Detective Roberts to Delaney's house. He took two or three other officers with him and they are going to search the entire area in and around his home, woods and all. I know it's been a long time, but maybe we'll luck out and find something."

"I want to caution you not to get your hopes up. Hopefully, before this evening is over we'll have some information. Whether it will be useful or not, we will just have to wait and see. I just wanted to tell you in person I messed up and I am sorry."

"Bob, before we eat I do have something to say." Chloe said.

Detective Bonner tensed, he knew that if he had followed through with his intuition then, this might not be happening to Chloe now.

"First of all, Bob, we are friends, but most of all we are Christians. We do forgive you. We all mess up from time to time so let's put that behind us." When Chloe finished her statement, the detective let out a sigh of relief. Chloe then began to tell Detective Bonner about her last couple of days.

When she finished, Chloe pulled out her list so she could give it to the detective and he could see the evidence of what she had been telling him.

"I know it's not very official. The time lines are just feelings and maybe's, but each one of those times I felt threatened. I also know you probably can't use this list now, but maybe somewhere in the future it will help you connect the dots. I'm going to continue to document these times and we'll see if it helps or not."

"One other thing, I've decided to take a self-defense class. It started this morning and I really do like it."

"Chloe, that is a great idea." Julie said, as she finally entered the conversation that was going on around her. "I think that is something I would be interested in. If you will call me later with the information, maybe I can sign up for the same class."

"Okay. I am hungry now. Let's eat." Seth said as Julie left to go get their daughter, Tiffany. Tiffany hadn't been feeling good so she was a little cranky. She had been playing on the floor just inside the patio door completely within Julie's sight. Bobby Jr. had gone to spend the night with his grandmother.

Detective Bonner went to get the hamburgers, Chloe went to get the chips, drinks and beans, and Seth went to help Chloe. Once everything was placed on the table and the blessing said, everyone begin to relax and just enjoy each other's company.

When it came time for them to leave, Seth and Chloe felt more relaxed than they had for several days. It felt good. Unknown to both the Kelley's and the Bonner's. A man sat watching as both couples came out from behind the house walking toward the Kelley's car.

This was the first time he had gotten a good look at Detective Bonner's wife. Maybe after dealing with Chloe it might be interesting to -------------no, no. She was a detective's wife. That wouldn't be to smart. But, she was a looker.

CHAPTER 11

C hloe sat on the patio. Seth had already left for work. She was just sitting there enjoying the peace and quiet. At times, she wondered if her stalker was out there watching her, but she didn't think so. She could usually tell. But, you just never knew.

It was such a nice morning. She knew Julie got up early with Tiffany so she decided to call and give her the information on the self-defense class. She was glad she was going to sign up. It would be nice to have somebody she knew in her class.

Chloe called Julie and gave her all the information she needed. Julie said she would call later after they had opened for business. It was early and Tiffany began to cry so Julie had to go.

Later on in the morning Julie called back saying she had made arrangements to take the same class as Chloe. She also asked Chloe if she wanted to make plans to do something either before or after their class. They talked for awhile, but Tiffany decided her mom had been on the phone long enough and she needed some of her attention. Especially a clean diaper.

———

He was angry at himself. He had overslept this morning and he hadn't gotten to his favorite tree in time to watch Chloe. He stood there watching as she picked up a book, the phone, and a coffee cup. When she had them safely settled into her hands, she went into the house.

It made him angrier still to know she had probably been out there all morning and he had been in his apartment sleeping. What a waste.

―――――

As Chloe straightened up the house, she thought about her time on the patio. She had not felt her stalkers presence, but she had felt God's.

The morning passed as the peace and quiet surrounded her. She had sat and watched the squirrels, listened to the birds and watched as a couple of deer grazed by slowly in front of her. They had looked at her and then gone on about their business.

The peace she felt was the peace that only God could give. The peace that surpassed all understanding. As it surrounded her, she had simply laid back and enjoyed God's comforting arms.

She knew others would not understand her relationship with God, but she didn't really care. Sometimes she didn't understand it either, but she knew He was there and that was all that mattered.

Chloe returned to the patio. She picked up the hose and started watering the plants. She decided to sit down, but once again, the peace she had been enjoying all morning was gone. She knew he was back.

She was through anyway so she turned the hose off and went back into the house. She had wanted to stay outside longer, but now she knew that wasn't going to happen.

She stood back out of the way so she couldn't be seen as she stared into the darkness of the woods behind the house. She wondered if he was out there watching her. She believed he was so she began to write in her book.

How she could so quickly change from one feeling to another baffled her. She was afraid. She tried not to be, but she was. She tried hard to contain this fear and there were times when she thought she had. But now, right this minute, fear overpowered her senses. She and Seth had decided just a few days ago to 'trust and lean' as it says in Proverbs 3:5.

She knew Jesus told us not to be afraid because He would be with us always. Chloe also knew that could mean she could live and be with Him or she could die and go to be with Him. Either way she would be with Him, but she wasn't quite ready to leave this earthly life.

Chloe had straightened up every room and now she was ready to vacuum those same rooms.

"Lord, am I going to die this time?" It was easy to vacuum while she talked to God. It made time pass faster and it was time well spent.

"I am so sorry I am afraid. I try so hard to trust and lean, but sometimes it gets really, really hard. I believe, oh, Lord, help my unbelief. Amen."

———

He leaned against the tree watching the patio door. He couldn't make up his mind whether to leave or not. Sometimes she would come back outside and work in the garden. He had periodically seen her as she cleaned and then vacuumed.

It was a cool day so he decided to wait for a while and hope for the best. As he leaned against the tree waiting for her to come out, he starting thinking about the night Sean had died. He was mad at him, but it had served him right.

It had served them both right. In the beginning they had both done what they had been told to do. Then they had decided to go out on their own. He didn't know if the police thought Sean Delaney had killed John Bledsoe or not. But, he knew.

Thankfully when Chloe had been rescued, Delaney had been in no shape to tell anyone anything. Death had a way of doing that to you. Now it was his turn. He just hadn't figured out how he was going to accomplish it. Things had been going his way and he had had some good ideas. He would just have to wait and see.

———

The next morning Chloe again went out and sat down to enjoy the peace and quiet. She decided she would call Julie, but Julie had some errands she needed to take care of so Chloe picked up a book deciding to read for a while. But as she sat there reading, she knew there was no peace and quiet for her today. He was there. She could feel it.

"What to do? What to do?" Chloe thought to herself. She needed to alert Detective Bonner to the fact that he was here, but she didn't want to alert 'him' to the fact she knew he was there. "Oh, God. I need some help. Please!"

Just then Chloe's cell phone rang. It was Seth.

"Hi, Chloe. I just had a few minutes so I thought I would see how your day was going?"

Chloe had to work really hard to keep the fear she felt from showing.

"Hi, Seth." Chloe said, as she listened for a bit and then said, "I'm sure you took those papers with you. I can go look if you want me to. I'm just sitting out on the patio. It won't take me anytime at all."

Seth stopped talking and started listening. "Chloe, he's out there. Isn't he?"

"Yes, your right there."

"Should I call Detective Bonner?"

"I think that would probably be a really good idea. What time do you want to go?"

Chloe was silent as she once again listened to Seth.

"Chloe, how are you holding up. Detective Bonner is on his way. He said if you thought you could do it, keep him there as long as you possibly can. Do you think you can do it?"

"Sure, do you want me to go look for them?"

"Chloe, I know this is hard, but if you can keep him there, our chances of catching him are pretty good."

"Give me an idea of where you think they might be."

Again Chloe waited, she pretended Seth was saying something to her while she listened to what he was saying. In reality he was helping to keep her calm by just talking to her.

It was hard to keep up a conversation that made no sense at all. For no matter what Chloe said, Seth's answer was not even close to what they were discussing.

"I think we have dragged this on long enough without him getting suspicious."

"You're probably right there."

"Okay, Chloe. It's time to get up and go in the house. Make sure you let him know you went to find my papers."

"Okay," Chloe said, as she got up from the chair and at the same time asked Seth, "Where do you want me to look?"

Chloe got up, walked in the house and locked the door behind her in one swift movement. She had become very adept at shutting and locking the door at the same time. So adept in fact you really couldn't tell whether she had just shut it or shut it and locked it.

When she got in the house, Chloe was able to ask Seth if he knew how close Detective Bonner was.

"Hold on, I've got him on the other phone. He said he just passed the road that turns off and goes in front of our house. He'll come to the front. The other police officers will turn off and go to the back.

"That sounds really good to me, Seth." she said, as she began to cry.

"You're fine, Chloe. Detective Bonner is pulling up in the front yard right now." Seth said, wishing he could be there.

Chloe ran out the front door and collided with the detective.

"Get in my car, Chloe. Lock the doors and don't get out until I come back." Detective Bonner ran right past her through the house and onto the patio. His eyes continually searching for someone. He came up empty.

The police coming from the other direction also came up empty. While they stood there deciding what to do next, they heard a motorcycle start up in the distance. But since the Kelley's lived in sort of a valley, they could not pin point the direction of the motor.

The police and the detective met in the center of the woods behind the house. Neither one having anything to show for their effort.

On the way back to the Kelley's house, Detective Bonner spotted a candy wrapper. He stooped, picked it up and placed it in the small baggie that he kept in his pocket for times such as this. He then headed toward the house. He went around to the front to get Chloe out of the car. She was still talking to Seth, but when she saw the detective she hung up and got out of the car.

"How are you doing, Chloe?"

"I've been better. Seth's on his way home, but he won't be here for a little while."

"That's okay. It will give us time to go over what has been happening to you this morning."

Detective Bonner and Chloe went in the house, but before they sat down to take care of business she asked him if he would like a cup of coffee. Or anything else to drink.

"Maybe in a little while, Chloe. First, we need to get your statement while it is fresh in your memory."

So Chloe started to tell him about her morning. From talking to Julie until he pulled up in front of the house. By the time she had finished telling him what had happened and he had asked her numerous questions Seth arrived.

He walked through the front door saying, "Did you catch him?"

"I'm afraid not. He left just before we got here. I don't know what alerted him, but Chloe you did a great job keeping him here as long as you did. I did find a candy wrapper. Hopefully, we'll get some evidence off of it."

As the police finished combing the area and Detective Bonner completed his uncomfortable task of questioning Chloe, they heard a motorcycle in the distance.

"It sounds like it's down by the mailbox." Seth said.

All three rushed out just in time to see someone pop-a-wheelie on his motorcycle and then take off. Detective Bonner ran to his car and drove down the driveway just as fast as he could.

The ruts in the road from the house to the mailbox were quite deep. It was only when the detective got to the mailbox that he could go a little faster, but even then their road wasn't the best. He tried, but he figured by then whoever it was had pulled off on one of the many side roads between the Kelley's house and the highway.

Upset with himself, he returned to the Kelley's to let them know he had failed once again, but as he passed the mailbox, he noticed the door was down and a note was hanging from it. He stopped, pulled up beside the mailbox and reached out to pick the note up very carefully.

"NICE TRY, MRS. KELLEY."

Detective Bonner drove back to the house. He couldn't make up his mind whether to show them the note or not, but when he pulled up in front of their garage and started to get out of the car, the first thing out of their mouths was, "What did you find at the mailbox?"

He reluctantly showed them.

"What do we do now, Detective?"

CHAPTER 12

The man had avoided the woods behind the Kelley's house for several days now. The police had almost caught him and "she" was the one who had laid the trap. So calm and so cool. It was time for him to think of a new plan. The woods had been great in the beginning, but now they were becoming too dangerous.

He had taken his brother's motorcycle back early this morning and picked up his own car. The distance between her house and town had not been an issue in the beginning, but now it was becoming a down right pain in the neck. What had seemed like fate working on his behalf now seemed to be working against him. Distance had become the biggest issue for him.

Dawn was beginning to break as the man once again drove in front of her house. He knew if she was going to be outside, she would be sitting on the back patio drinking her coffee or she would be working in the yard somewhere in the back of the house. He drove to the end of the road then turned around. After driving in front of the house one more time, he headed for town. He was hungry and decided to go to Taco Bell before heading for home.

He was really angry at her for the stunt she had pulled the last time he had been watching her. She had played the game well that day. So well, in fact, the police had almost caught him. Now, he would have to find a different way to play.

━━━━━━━━━

Chloe had left earlier that morning. She and Julie were going to Taco Bell for breakfast before they headed to their self-defense class. Both Chloe and Julie pulled into the parking lot at the same time. They parked side by side, pulled the keys out of the ignition, reached over in the seat beside them to get their purses, stepped out and locked the car door behind them, and then turned heading toward the entrance to Taco Bell all at the same time.

They both laughed as once again they said good morning at the same time. Walking through the front door they approached the counter. After they placed their order, paid for it, and then picked it up, they looked around for a place to sit.

"I guess we can sit wherever we want to. There is hardly anyone here," Chloe said, as she tried to decide where to sit. "Why don't we sit over in the corner. That way we can talk and not bother anyone else. That is if anyone comes in."

As they talked, they both noticed a handsome young man come in and place his order. When he was finished and had his food in his hand, he came and sat down on a seat just two seats away from them. They looked at each other with upraised eyebrows. It seemed strange that with all the empty seats around them he would pick one so close.

Once again Chloe and Julie started talking and soon forgot the young man seated beside them.

"Julie," Chloe said, making sure she had her friend's attention.

Looking at Chloe with a questioning glance, she said, "What?"

"Would you and Bob be interested in going on our church trip?"

"I thought only members of the church could go."

"Most of them are from the church, but there are some that ask their personal friends to go along. And I am asking you. What do you think?"

"Where and when?"

"It's September 26th through September 30th. We are going to Broken Bow, Oklahoma. We will be meeting in the parking lot on the right hand side of the street as you're entering town. I think it's across from some church. We are meeting at 7:00 a.m. We'll gather there then more or less have a caravan. That's all I know for right now, but if you're interested, I'll send you an email with the rest of the information."

"It sounds like fun. I'll have to ask Bob and see if he has any time off."

"But right now, we need to get going or we are going to be late for our class." As she stood up, she held her stomach. "I am really, really full. I'm not sure eating just before class was a good idea.

"I agree. But, maybe we can work it off in class."

Chloe and Julie got their stuff together and walked out to their cars.

"Chloe, before we leave how are things going with your stalker?" Julie asked her friend seriously.

"Right now it seems pretty good. I haven't felt his presence for a while. Actually I haven't felt anything since the police almost caught him. Maybe, he has decided I'm not worth the trouble. Wouldn't that be great?"

"Yes, that would be great. Now let's get to class before we're late."

———

The man smiled to himself as he watched Chloe and Julie get into two separate cars and leave. He had just decided he was going to go on vacation, too. He had all the information he needed. He would join the caravan. His destination: Broken Bow, Oklahoma.

———

Julie stopped Chloe as they both approached the door to their self-defense class. "Chloe, what do you think about asking M. Brown if he would teach a shortened version of our class. Say once or twice a week for a month. Some people can't afford classes that never end, but if they were able to attend for a specific amount of time and for a specified amount of money, they might be more apt to commit. I think it would be really beneficial. I know it has been for me. What do you think?"

"I really hadn't thought about it. I do know it gives me a self-confidence that I haven't felt before. I have more information that helps keep me safe when I'm by myself. Like locking the doors immediately after getting in the car. Not after I'm through balancing my checkbook. Julie, I think it's a great idea. Let's talk to M. Brown after class."

After entering the room, they started doing some stretching exercises while they waited for the class to begin. Today's class was one of the more strenuous ones and they had begun regretting going to Taco Bell before class.

After class was over, they were both sitting on the edge of their mats waiting for M. Brown to come back into the room.

They weren't allowed to wear their shoes inside the teaching area so there they sat. Waiting. Since they knew M. Brown also taught in Livingston, Chloe had changed her class to Livingston and Julie had just signed up there. It was closer for Julie to attend and it wasn't that much farther for Chloe to drive. They had just about given up when he walked back into the room.

"What are you two still doing here?"

"We thought we would like to get your opinion on something and to see if it was possible to do." Julie said, as she stood up and began to tell M. Brown her idea. When she finished, she looked at his face to see if she could tell what he was thinking. It didn't look promising.

"What brought this about?"

Julie looked at Chloe, "Chloe, is it alright if I tell him?" M. Brown looked at Chloe questioningly as she nodded her head yes. Then Julie began to tell him about Chloe's stalker and how he was the reason Chloe had started taking the class in the first place. Once Chloe had started, Julie decided she wanted to take the class, too. With all that they had gained from the class, they wanted to be able to share it with others. Julie ended with saying, "A lot of women can't afford the money or the time for a regular class, but if you were able to teach a class that was only once or twice a week for a month for a specified amount, that would be great. If you say yes, I'll see what I can set up with my church."

"I'll see what I can do. It does sound like a good idea, but I am really busy right now. I'm sorry, Chloe, I didn't know what was going on in your life, but I will try my best to work something out."

"Thank you," both Chloe and Julie said at the same time. They both sat down and began putting on their shoes. After talking to M. Brown, they decided they were too tired to go shopping so they separated and each one ran their own errands then headed for home.

CHAPTER 13

The man stood in the shadows as he waited for her car to arrive. Smiling to himself, he sat in the darkness just watching and waiting.

The parking lot was empty, but that was to be expected. He was early. He was hoping the plan had not changed in so far as meeting in the parking lot and driving in a caravan to their destination because he had chosen to give Chloe's stalking a rest. He wanted Chloe to think he had moved on so maybe she would lower her defenses. So with little to go on, he had decided he would just see what happened. If he couldn't find her, he would just take a vacation and maybe find someone else. Who knew?

While he stood there, he saw the first vehicle pull into the parking lot. He quickly moved back into the shadows making sure he could not be seen. The lights from the car illuminated him in their harsh glow for just a moment. He stumbled as he tried to get out of the way.

After picking himself up, he watched Chloe pull the pickup's tailgate down then sit on it while she waited for Seth to finish what he was doing. He could hear them talking and laughing as they waited for the others to show up.

Just then another car pulled into the parking lot. They pulled in right beside Seth and Chloe and stopped. A man and woman got out and went over to talk to them as they waited for the others to arrive. One by one the other vehicles began to arrive and within thirty minutes everyone was there.

Everyone greeted everyone else then at long last it was time to go. After the first car drove out onto the deserted street, all the other cars began to follow. The caravan was now on its way to Broken Bow, Oklahoma.

He backed out of his parking space and as quick as he could, pulled in behind the last car of the caravan. Keeping it in sight he could not help but laugh out loud. This was going to be a very interesting trip.

The man followed the caravan closely. He didn't want to lose anyone. Thankfully he had taken the precaution of writing down the license numbers of each car plus the make and model as each one pulled into the parking lot.

It was a good thing he had taken that precaution because as they drove north different ones in the caravan would drop out to look at different things along the way. He had made several wrong turns by following the wrong car. The cars always came back and joined the caravan, but it took him out of the way. It also made him nervous because at first he didn't know if they would rejoin the caravan or not.

After taking the wrong turn twice, the man decided to find Chloe's pickup and stay with it. He was tired and he was getting low on gas. What he was going to do if he had to leave the caravan and get gas wasn't a big concern because he knew where they were going, but he preferred to follow them.

Once again the man looked at his gas gauge. It was just above the empty mark. He had no choice. He was going to have to

stop. He saw the gas station sign up ahead and put on his turn signal. Then watched as each member of the caravan began putting on their turn signal and exiting the highway. He was ecstatic as he pulled up to the pump and began pumping gas. When his car was full, he pulled forward so another car could pull in behind him. He got out and went inside the convenience store thinking he would get himself something to snack on.

There stood Chloe. She was looking at some t-shirts. They had crossed the Oklahoma State line so all the shirts had something to do with Oklahoma. The man went over and stood beside Chloe as he pretended to be looking at the t-shirts, too. He was so close he could smell her perfume.

"Chloe, are you going to get a shirt or not? Everyone is checking out and getting ready to leave." Seth asked.

"I can't make up my mind, Seth. I really like this one," Chloe said, as she held up a blue, pink, and purple tie dyed t-shirt. It had shiny beads on the back that surrounded the outline of the state. On the front it also had some shiny beads placed here and there.

"But, I also like this one. I just can't make up my mind."

"Why don't you just get both of them. I'm finished, so I'll wait for you outside."

"Okay." Chloe said, as she put both t-shirts back on the rack. She headed toward the door meeting some of the other women that were leaving at the same time. Talking and laughing one by one they went through the door.

The man watched while each member of the group got into their car. One by one they pulled into a line off to the side of the station so they wouldn't block the flow of traffic then they stopped and waited until everyone was ready. When the last car got in line, it was time for the caravan to head north. The man pulled in behind the last car. Now he could relax a little. Chloe was close to the front of the line, but he didn't want her to even get a hint that she was being watched. He had decided that if someone turned off and they were no longer headed north, he would just find one of the other cars and follow it. He had his drink, he had a snack, he had a tank full of gas so he settled in for the drive north to Broken Bow, Oklahoma.

CHAPTER 14

F inally, he was almost there. The sign as he entered the town said Broken Bow. He continued to follow the caravan, but he did pull up closer to the front. Not that he was afraid of losing them, but he really wanted to arrive at the same time they did. He was hoping that the front desk would include him in the group just by sight, not by actually checking in with them. If it would work, he didn't know, but it was worth a try.

The lodge was right in front of him. He had been so deep in thought he really hadn't been paying much attention and now he was here. The cars in front were pulling into the parking spaces so he pulled in right beside them. As he got out of his car, he noticed that the other cars were all following suit.

The members of the caravan got out of their cars, stopped and began talking to one another. While talking, they slowly ambled toward the front office. The man got out of his car just as Chloe and Seth were walking by. When she heard the car door shut, Chloe glanced in the direction of the sound and smiled at the man getting out of the car. After saying a quick hi, she went back to talking to the couple walking beside them.

They were all congregating in small groups talking while waiting for Tammy to check them in. She would hand out the keys to each room once she had accomplished her task. It was so much easier for her to check them in rather than having everyone standing around the check-in counter at one time checking themselves in. So the man was able to pass them. He walked slowly toward the office. He hadn't really wanted to be one of the first to go in. He wanted to blend in, but after passing Chloe and heading that way he couldn't think of an alternative.

He could feel her eyes watching him, but just then another car pulled into the parking area. They parked several feet past the sidewalk that turned off heading toward the office. So instead of walking toward the office he went straight and walked toward the car. He had always had the gift of gab so when the other couple got out of their car, he walked up and started talking to them. He knew it would look like they were meeting here and hoped that Chloe would think that, too.

———

Chloe watched as the man passed her on the sidewalk. She and Seth were talking to some of the members of their caravan, but she felt him as he walked by. It wasn't a good feeling. He was a handsome man. Friendly. She also had the feeling she had seen him somewhere before, but couldn't place where.

She watched as he headed toward the office. Then instead of turning and following the sidewalk, he abruptly changed direction and turned toward a car that had just pulled into an empty parking space. He went over and started talking to the couple after they got out of their car and stepped up on the sidewalk.

She couldn't tell whether it looked as if they were friends or not, but since she had been coping with her stalker for such a long period of time, she had become overly suspicious of certain actions that she would not have given a second thought to before.

"Chloe, are you listening?" Seth asked, as he grabbed hold of her hand pulling her toward the office. "We need to go get our key from Tammy so we can go and unpack the pickup. Once we're unpacked, we're going to meet down by the lake and have a picnic. Let's go so we can get finished and then see if we can help."

"Okay, Okay. I guess my mind was somewhere else."

"No kidding. I had to say your name three times before you answered me."

"Chloe, why don't you go talk to some of the other ladies and I'll get the key. As soon as I have it, we'll find where the room is then go to the pickup and grab our stuff."

"Okay, that sounds like a plan to me."

Chloe found some of the other women in their group and started talking. Their husbands went to get their keys, so some of the women decided to go look around while waiting. They walked past the check in counter and went through the double doors going into the lounge/eating area. There was a fireplace with a couple of couches and a few chairs set in front of it. Behind the couches were several tables set up with chairs at each one. Then off to the side was a microwave and a coffee pot. Going through some French doors on the other side of the room was a very large patio with several tables and chairs looking out over the lake.

"Chloe, come on. I've got the keys. Let's go get our stuff and put it in our room. Once we find it, that is."

Just as Chloe and Seth left to find their room the man entered the office going straight to the check-in counter to get in line. When it was his turn, he smiled at the young girl behind the counter as he asked the question, "I know this is last minute, but I am hoping you have a room I can rent?"

"Yes, sir. We do." She said, as she studied the book in front of her. "How about Room 163?"

"That's fine with me." He said, flirting with the girl a little. He figured she might come in handy later and she was cute. "I appreciate your help and I will be seeing you later."

The girl smiled at the handsome young man as he walked away from the counter in the direction of his room.

CHAPTER 15

Chloe sat on the balcony of their room early the next morning. The sun was beginning to come up making its way over the mountain tops. It was a bright orange and it was breathtakingly beautiful. Each of the rooms had a balcony and they all faced the lake.

This time of the morning was Chloe's 'God Time.' She loved this time because as the day dawned, it felt all fresh and new. She continued to watch the sun climb higher into the sky and she could not hold back the words of love she felt for her God. When the sun reached a certain point, the orange glow of its rays traveled across the lake slowly making their way from one side to the other. The rays broke in the middle of the lake for an island, but then started up once again on the other side. They continued on until they finally stopped at the shoreline right in front of her. It was a beautiful sight to behold. Chloe just stood there taking in the beauty of the moment.

White clouds danced around the sun with each one having its tips covered with an orange glow. Chloe was transfixed by the beauty that surrounded her. She didn't want to move. She wanted this moment to last forever. Then from the edge of the trees her eyes saw a movement and as she turned in that direction, five deer made their way out of the trees. She watched them as they slowly made their way from one side of her vision to the other. It was then she saw the figure of a man. He just stood there watching her.

"Oh, God, Please, not now. How can this be? Surely, it can't be?" Chloe questioned herself, as she stood there. She didn't want to move, but she didn't want to stay there either. She wanted to go back into their room, but she stood there paralyzed. She didn't want to believe that her stalker actually had the ability to find out where she was going and to follow her there.

Chloe tried hard to look deep into the shadows caused by the trees, but she could no longer see anything. The sun continued to rise, but Chloe's peace was gone. She hated to leave and go back into the room, but now she felt exposed.

"Seth, wake up. I need to talk to you." Chloe said, walking over to his side of the bed. She hated to wake him up, but she really needed to talk to him. "Seth, please, wake up."

"What is it, Chloe?" Seth asked his wife.

"Seth, I need to talk to you."

"Can you wait until I get fully awake?"

"Sure. If you hurry up."

"What's the rush, Chloe?"

"You'll understand in a minute. Just get up. Please?"

Seth got up and went into the bathroom grumbling. He wasn't ready to get up yet.

Chloe could hear Seth in the bathroom. When he brushed his teeth, she knew he was almost ready. The bathroom door finally opened and out came Seth.

"Okay, Chloe. What is going on? I was looking forward to sleeping in this morning."

"Oh, Seth, I don't even know where to begin."

"At the beginning would be nice."

"Seth, listen. He's here."

"Who's here?"

"Seth, pay attention. He's here. The stalker is here."

"How can he be here? Are you sure?"

"I'm not positive if that's what you mean. But you know what I'm talking about."

"I know. Let's go get a cup of coffee in the lounge first so I have time to wake up and let it sink in. Then we'll talk about it. Okay?"

They both finished getting dressed and went downstairs. Laughter greeted them from the lounge so after getting their coffee, they decided to sit and talk with the others for a little while finding out what the day's schedule was going to be. As they sat talking to their friends, Chloe's stress level slowly disappeared. Then she began to second guess herself deciding maybe she had just over reacted to seeing someone in the woods. Forgetting completely what Detective Bonner had told her about paying attention to those same feelings.

"Chloe, would you like some more coffee?"

"Sure," she said, as she held out her empty coffee cup.

"Do we still need to go for a walk so we can talk?" Seth whispered, while at the same time picking Chloe's cup up, giving her a kiss on the cheek then heading toward the coffee pot.

"No, it's okay."

"What are you two whispering about?" Tammy asked, as she approached to tell them good morning. Tammy was the one that had put the trip together. She had scouted out ahead of time things for them to do, plus she had planned all of their activities. She was really good at organizing and Chloe wished that she had that same ability. Organization. It was definitely not one of Chloe's talents.

"Seth and I were trying to decide whether we were going to go for a walk now or later. I told him we should probably wait until later."

"That's good because after we finish with breakfast, the girls are going antiquing and the boys are going fishing. Does Seth like to fish?" Tammy asked.

Seth returned with Chloe's cup of coffee and as he sat it on the table in front of her, he turned and told Tammy, "I'm not much of a fisherman, but I do like to explore. I always like to check out my surroundings when I'm in a new place. So if you hear of anybody that would rather explore than fish, let me know."

The group as a whole had a full day in front of them. Some of the men had already left to go fishing. Some were just getting their stuff ready to go. The women were still sitting and discussing what time they were going to leave. Finally Tammy stood up and said "OK, everybody. Let's go. We have a catered B-B-Q this evening so if we want to get finished with our antiquing, we better get this show on the road." Tammy headed to her room to get what she needed for an antiquing trip. Then she would join the ladies out front.

Seth headed toward their room while Chloe turned toward the office door intending to join the other ladies out front where they were going to decide who was going to ride with whom. As Chloe opened the door, she glanced back at the check in counter to tell the girl who was working there goodbye. The man she saw yesterday on their arrival was standing there flirting with her.

Even though the man was flirting with the girl at the counter, he was watching Chloe. She thought the girl's name was Sandy, but she wasn't sure. Because Sandy was flirting, too, Chloe went on through the door without saying anything.

"God, am I being paranoid?" Chloe asked herself, as she headed to the parking lot.

CHAPTER 16

Seth stood staring at the door in front of him. On the door hung the two t-shirts Chloe had been looking at when they stopped to fill up with gas just after entering Oklahoma. He knew Chloe had decided not to get either one of them, but now they were both hanging on the door to their room.

"What is going on?" Seth thought to himself, but at the same time he was afraid he knew.

He turned around looking at the parking lot. The girls must have decided who was riding with whom because they were all getting into the cars. Seth's first thought was to stop Chloe and tell her what he had just found, but he decided to wait because he didn't want to ruin her day.

Seth sat on the bed and leaned over putting his head in his hands. "Maybe there is a reasonable explanation and I am simply jumping to the wrong conclusion. Maybe someone in our group is playing a practical joke on one or both of us." As much as he wanted to believe it was someone playing a joke on them, he really didn't believe it.

He walked to the door of the balcony. Looking toward the lake he prayed, "God, what am I going to do? What are we going to do? I feel so helpless."

———————

The man talked Sandy into showing him around town. He had heard Chloe's group talk about going antiquing. He didn't really know what that was, but when he heard the word resale shop, he asked Sandy if there were some and where they were. Broken Bow wasn't a large town and he figured he could find them. Sandy got off at noon so she volunteered to go with him and show him around. He hadn't really planned on it, but when opportunity knocks at the door, he wasn't one to turn it down. He was here on a mission so he took Sandy's hand and off they went.

———————

Chloe was looking at some t-shirts in one of the shops. She heard someone laugh and turned around to see who it was. It was Sandy and the man at the counter.

"God, please tell me this is a coincidence," she said, as she looked at the man. Instead of looking at Sandy he was watching her. Antiquing no longer interested her. She saw some of the girls sitting outside on some benches so she decided to join them.

Chloe sat there quietly listening to the conversation going on around her. Her mind deep in thought. "Could someone really have followed her all the way up here? Because, if he did????" Chloe stopped there because she had no answer to the question.

Just then, Mina Fae interrupted Chloe's thoughts by saying "Chloe, we're going to go ahead and leave. The others are almost through so they won't be far behind us. Do you want to go with us or wait for the others to finish checking out?"

"I think I'll go with ya'll." Chloe said quickly. She wanted to get as far away from the man in the store as humanly possible and as quick as possible. "Whose car are we going in?"

"I'm ready to go, too, so why don't we go in mine." Tammy suggested. "Let me tell the ones still in the store and then we'll be off."

Tammy put her head in the door and yelled, "Hey, Glenda! Five of us are leaving now. So could you tell the ones still in the store we'll meet them back at the lodge and to be sure and count heads so no one is left behind."

"That's okay, Tammy. I think everyone has checked out and the ones inside are just looking around. I'll let them know. Where are we going now?" Glenda asked.

"I think we better go back to the lodge, relax for a little while, then get ready for tonight's B-B-Q. I have to leave early to meet the caterer at the pavilion." Tammy said, as she walked toward her car. "Is everyone here? If we are, let's go." She said, while getting into her car and turning around to make sure all those who were riding with her were in the car and buckled in. Seeing that everyone was there she proceeded to back out of the parking lot and pull out on the highway once again driving through Broken Bow. As she pulled out onto the highway, the other cars fell in line behind her.

Chloe sat quietly in the back seat listening to everyone talk, but she didn't really feel like participating. She couldn't wait to get back to the lodge. She was tired and she really needed to talk to Seth.

The man stood in front of the store watching as Chloe's caravan left. He didn't have to follow her now. He knew where she was going.

When the girls returned, they found several of the men were already there. The discussion then began on who had caught the biggest fish. Laugher broke out as the story was told on one of the men who had fallen into the river not once, not twice but three times.

"Has anyone seen Seth?" Chloe asked, as she approached the men who were elaborating on their fishing stories.

"No, but we just pulled in and parked." Con said.

"Thanks, I'll go see if I can find him. See ya'll later. What time are we leaving for the pavilion?" Chloe asked.

"I have to be there at 5:00 p.m. to help the caterers set up. If anyone wants to go at the same time, that's fine with me." Tammy said, turning toward Chloe. "We need to meet in the lounge at 4:30 p.m. I already know how to get there, so those who want to, can follow me."

"See you at 4:30 p.m. Seth and I will follow you because unless Seth scouted it out and found it today, we have no idea where we're going." Chloe said, then turned and started walking toward her room.

Chloe had forgotten her key, as usual, so she knocked on the door then stood waiting for Seth to let her in. When Seth opened the door, he reached out and gave Chloe a bear hug pulling her into the room. "How was your day?"

"Pretty good. Other than being a little tired I'm fine. How was yours? You know what I was going to do. What did you end up doing?" Chloe asked, as she followed Seth into the room.

Seth led her to the balcony where they sat down in the two chairs located there.

"Chloe, you and I need to talk for a minute."

"What about?"

"When I came back to the room to get ready to go explore, I found these two shirts hanging on our door. Do you recognize them?"

As she looked at the shirts, Chloe's heart did a nose dive. She could hardly breathe. "Seth, please tell me you bought me those shirts."

"Chloe, you know I didn't. I left before you did, and you're not listening. I said they were hanging on the door when I came back. I don't know if you were the one who was supposed to find them or not. I am actually glad that you didn't."

"Should we leave, Seth? Should we just pack our bags and go home?"

"I hate to say this, but I don't think it's going to matter one way or the other."

"Well, do we at least tell our friends what we think is going on?" Chloe asked, as she waited for Seth's answer. When he didn't answer her right away, she began to cry. They stayed that way for several minutes not moving. Finally, Chloe stood up and wiped her eyes. Seth stood up behind her and they walked back into their room closing the balcony door behind them.

———

The man smiled as he sat on the little balcony below them. His flirtation with Sandy was paying off. Once he had discovered the room below Chloe was empty, he talked Sandy into letting him change rooms. Even if Seth and Chloe left, he had decided he was going to stay for awhile. After all he had a life, too.

Chloe and Seth laid on the bed. He held her close to him hoping she would fall asleep. But the tenseness of her body told him she was laying there with her eyes wide open.

Seth woke with a start. When he looked at the clock, he was surprised to find that both he and Chloe had fallen asleep. He was sure it was something they both needed but now it was time to meet the others downstairs.

"Chloe, wake up. We better get ready to go."

Chloe opened her eyes and turned to look at him while at the same time moving to get off the bed. She walked toward the bathroom to freshen up and as she passed her husband, she stopped to ask him the question that had been on their minds before they fell asleep.

"Seth, what are we going to do?"

"To tell you the truth. I don't know. I really don't know."

After they had both freshened up, they grabbed their jackets and walked downstairs to the lounge area where they were meeting everyone else who was following Tammy to the pavilion. But just before Seth's hand touched the door knob, he stepped back into the room taking hold of Chloe's hands. "Chloe, we need to pray."

"You're right, Seth. Sometimes I lose sight of the very One that can help me."

"I know. I've done it before, too. But now I feel very strongly in my heart that this is exactly what we are supposed to do."

Chloe and Seth faced each other as Seth began to pray. "Lord, we come before You with troubled hearts. To tell You the truth, our minds are consumed with fear. We don't want to feel that way, but we do. You know what is going on and You know

100

the outcome. We trust You because we know You are walking by our side. Give us the strength to overcome this problem and please, Lord, don't take Chloe from me. Amen."

After Seth finished praying, he asked Chloe if there was anything she wanted to add.

"No, I think you've about covered it all." Chloe said, they both left the room hand in hand.

Everyone had decided to leave at the same time. If Tammy needed help, they would all be right there so they could pitch in.

"You know we have to tell them?" Seth said.

"Yes, I know. When?"

"Now is just as good of a time as any, I guess. Should we tell Brother Rodney first or just tell everyone at the same time."

"Let's tell everyone at the same time. I don't think I can go through it more than once." Chloe said, as they both took a deep breath and entered the room.

Tammy was telling everyone it was time to go. Seth walked over and whispered in her ear. When Seth finished, she looked at Chloe who had just finished closing the doors to the room.

"Hey, everybody. Quiet down. Seth has something he wants to say."

"Brother Rodney, we are certainly glad you are here. We are definitely going to need some prayer here in a little bit."

Everyone sat down and began to look questioningly at Seth. He proceeded to tell them what had been happening to Chloe over a period of time, but then he relayed what had just happened with the t-shirts. After he had relayed their story, his eyes traveled around the room as he looked each one in the eyes saying, "What each one of you need to decide is whether you want us to go or to stay. We will do whatever you decide and we will understand. We will leave in the morning if that is the decision."

Seth turned to Brother Rodney and asked, "Would you please lead us in prayer before we leave?"

Everyone stood and faced Brother Rodney as he began to pray. "Lord, this situation has come out of nowhere and should not be taken lightly. We are the children of the most high God and therefore we enjoy Your protection. While each one of us comes to terms with what is happening and has been happening to Chloe and Seth, may You guide us in the decision that is placed before us. Lord, we ask Your protection for each and everyone in this room. In Jesus' most Holy Name. Amen."

"Before everyone leaves I want you to know my position on this matter. I would prefer everyone to stand behind Chloe and Seth. I will do so. But, at the same time each one of you is free to make your own decision. So now Tammy I guess it's time for us to leave." Brother Rodney said, as he got up and headed toward the door.

"Thank you, Brother Rodney. Both Chloe and I appreciate your prayer and your decision." Seth said. "It's in God's hands now, Chloe." He took Chloe's hand in his and they both turned and walked toward the door.

Everyone got into their cars and drove toward the pavilion where the B-B-Q was to take place. It was still daylight, but in about thirty minutes or so, the sun would go down behind the mountains and darkness would prevail. Tonight Chloe was afraid of the dark and now so was everyone else.

The man sat and watched as the last couple went through the office door. Sandy was on duty so he walked up to the counter to talk to her.

"You seem to have an exodus on your hands." He said, hoping she would tell him where they were going.

"Yes, they reserved the pavilion. They are going to have a B-B-Q and a sing-a-long evidently." She said, as she watched two of the men carrying their guitars.

"You're almost off duty aren't you, Sandy? How would you like to go for a ride?"

"That would be great. Although, I still have ten minutes to go before I get off."

"That's okay. I'll wait. I'll be back in ten minutes."

"Great. See you later."

He knew he could get Sandy to show him where the pavilion was. He decided to walk down by the lake while he waited for Sandy to get off.

———

The pavilion was about five miles from the lodge. Chloe and Seth drove in silence each one deep in their own thoughts.

"It sure is quiet in here." Chloe broke the silence after they had been driving for several minutes.

"I'm thinking, Chloe. My thoughts are jumping around in my head and landing nowhere. What if they don't want us to stay? I know we will leave, but what will that decision do to our relationship with the church?"

"I don't know, Seth. This night is going to be an especially long night."

Seth looked at Chloe as he pulled into the parking lot. "Everyone is probably having this same conversation. I guess we'll just have to wait and see how it plays out. I know it's going to be a long night, but Chloe this has been a bombshell. And sometimes fear overrides anything else. We have already been through this. Time after time. They are just starting. Let's just go and try to have a good time. Okay!"

"Okay, Seth. Let's put on God's armour and step out in faith. It's especially true right now. It's funny how we sometimes forget how much we need that armor until something bad starts happening."

They met in front of the pickup. Seth took Chloe's hand and placed it in his then they began walking in the direction of the pavilion. The touching of their hands gave them the strength to take one more step not allowing 'the man' to win.

———

The man and Sandy had been driving around for about an hour when he asked Sandy, "How many pavilions are in this area, if I wanted to have a family reunion?"

"The closest one is just down the road."

"I am trying to get my family to get together and have a reunion and this seems like a really nice place."

"I can show you where it is, but we can't stop."

"Why not?"

"Remember the group that left the lodge right before us?"

"Yea."

"Well, that's the group that rented it and they have it rented for the whole evening."

The man smiled to himself as Sandy pointed it out. He could see Chloe sitting by Seth. They were talking to the couple sitting beside them seemingly to have forgotten he even existed. He would have to remedy that.

CHAPTER 17

The man sat quietly in the darkness watching the pavilion and all the people that were walking around having such a good time. He got as close as he could, but he didn't get close enough for anyone to be able to see him. He told Sandy he had to work. She was disappointed, but what could she say. She thought he was a writer and when the inspiration hit him, he needed to write. She wasn't too happy, but he took her home and then returned to the pavilion by himself.

As he stood there waiting for an opportunity to get close to Chloe, he noticed how much Sandy and Chloe looked alike. Maybe that was why he was drawn to Sandy. He knew she was hurt because he had cut their time together short, but he would make it up to her tomorrow.

After eating their B-B-Q, Chloe and Seth got up to mingle. They had decided it would be the best way to handle their situation. By talking to everyone, they would be giving each one the opportunity to tell them how they felt, but at the same time no one would know who said they would rather they didn't stay.

Lenny and Ruford had gone to get their guitars out of their cars. When they returned, they both sat down on a picnic table. This way they could balance their guitars on their laps while they sang. Tammy and Mina Fae went to stand beside the two men. Those who could carry a tune joined them as they all prepared to begin singing.

Chloe loved it whenever everyone got together to sing Christian songs. They sang long into the night and finally Tammy had to tell everyone it was time for them to go. As their last song of the evening, Lenny and Ruford started playing "Amazing Grace". The moment they began to sing, Tammy and Mina Fae joined in and then one by one the whole group began to sing. When the song came to an end, everyone started picking everything up and putting it in their cars or the trash. They also made sure the area was clean. Leaving it as clean, if not cleaner, than it was when they arrived.

With the sing-a-long breaking up and everyone finally getting in their cars to go back to the lodge, Chloe and Seth could almost breathe a sigh of relief because no one had mentioned anything about not wanting them to be with the group anymore. Chloe hoped that sentiment carried on into the next day. She knew she would be hurt, but she could also understand why they would feel that way. Understanding was one thing, but...

"Hey, Chloe!" Barry called out.

Her heart sank as she stopped and turned around to see what Barry wanted.

"You forgot your purse," he said, putting Chloe's purse in her hands.

"Thanks, Barry." Chloe said, while relief began to wash over her. When she had first heard his voice call her name, she had been afraid he was the one that was going to tell them to go. But when all he wanted to do was return her purse, Chloe could not contain the smile that welled up from within.

———

The man stood watching as Chloe and her husband got in their pickup. But, then they stopped. He continued standing in the darkness watching as those that were left began to get in their cars. He watched as the lights to the pavilion were turned off and the last couple, after making their way to their car, drove to the front of the line. Then each car pulled in behind them as they headed back to the lodge. He could see the red tail lights of the last car as it left the area. Though it was dark, there was enough light from the moon to be able to make his way to his car. When he located it, he got in and left following the caravan of cars back to the lodge. He was in no hurry. By morning he would be back in place. Watching and waiting.

———

No one had approached them while they were at the pavilion last night and they ended up having a really good time. The singing was her favorite part. She and Seth had mingled a lot because they had wanted to give everyone the opportunity to let them know how they were feeling.

On the ride back, she and Seth had talked about getting up in the morning and just leaving. When morning arrived, they still hadn't made a decision. They had thought about getting Brother Rodney off to the side and discussing it with him, but since they couldn't make up their mind, they decided that for now they would go down and eat breakfast.

As they walked into the Lounge/Breakfast room, they noticed everyone else was already there. Chloe and Seth both headed toward the coffee pot. Filling their cups, they turned around and faced the group.

"Is there something going on we should know about?" Seth asked, as he and Chloe found an empty place to sit. He sat down next to Chloe and they both looked around at everyone expectantly.

"I guess I have been elected as the spokesman for the group," Brother Rodney said, as he stood up facing Chloe and Seth. "We are not a courageous group, but we are a group that believes in Jesus. We've had a meeting, sort of anyway, and we formally want to ask you to stay."

They sat staring at Brother Rodney not knowing what to say. Chloe's eyes started filling with tears and Seth, well, Seth just sat there.

"We figured we might as well just get everything out in the open. We decided to go on as if nothing has happened on the outside, but on the inside we are to make sure Chloe is never alone. Someone will be with her at all times. I've heard this saying and I will probably completely mess it up, but it says something like this. For evil to abound, good men just have to do nothing. So we will do the best we can. What do you think about that?"

"Thank you," Seth answered. "You will probably never know how much this means to us. Thank you from the both of us."

Sandy's laughter from the counter made the short meeting come to an end. Everyone stood up and walked over to Seth and Chloe and either hugged or shook hands with them. Finally Tammy stood by the door and said, "Our first trip this morning, other than the guys going fishing that is, is to take it easy and just sit out on the patio. We can talk, play a few games, but mainly just get to know one another better. That is what this trip is really all about. To become more than acquaintances who just say hi at church and that's all. Let's actually become friends."

Knowing that the men were getting ready to go and the wives needed a potty break Tammy said, "Why don't we all meet back here in thirty minutes. That way you can say goodbye to your husbands and do whatever you need to do. Thirty minutes, ladies. Let's go."

Later, once their thirty minutes was up, the ladies began their exodus out of the lounge. They passed Sandy and her new beau just as he said "Sandy, I sure am sorry you have to work today. I was hoping you could show me around town some more. What time do you get off?"

"Four o'clock."

"Why don't I meet you here at four o'clock and we will go do something together? I am forever in your debt for showing me around town, so why don't I take you out somewhere nice for dinner to show you my appreciation?"

"It's been a pleasure showing you around, but I would also enjoy going out somewhere nice to eat. I'll meet you here at four."

"Great," the man said, as he turned and looked straight at Chloe and smiled.

Chloe walked out the door wondering what had just happened. Was she over reacting? Was he just being nice? As she put all the other things that had happened together, she didn't think so, but did she really know for sure?

"Oh, God!" Chloe thought to herself. "Is this never going to end?"

Tomorrow would be the last day for the girls to fit in that one final shopping trip. It would also be the last time the guys would be able to go fishing before going home. Although there were those that had decided to stay longer, most were going home as planned or going someplace else before returning home. All in all, it was a successful trip. Friends remained friends and new friends were made.

When they went shopping the next day, Chloe was never left alone. If it wasn't one of the women with her, it was Seth. Throughout the day, Chloe felt safe in everything she did and ended up enjoying the whole day. Everyone went out to eat that evening. This would be their last evening together. Since everyone enjoyed the sing-a-longs so much, everyone gathered out on the patio. The guys brought their guitars and the ones that could carry a tune sang with a little more gusto than the ones who couldn't carry a tune at all. They were all disappointed when it was time to go to bed. Their trip was officially over.

———

The man stood watching as Chloe's group started getting their things together for their exodus. They had a small continental type breakfast in the lounge. He joined the party, but sat off to the side watching as they said their goodbyes. They tried to include him, but he shook his head no and just continued to sip on his coffee. He wondered if they would be so nice if they realized who he was. They finally finished talking, they prayed for traveling mercies and then they all began to head for their cars. He wondered if they really believed that all the praying they did, really helped.

———

Chloe and Seth had tried to keep their problem from affecting anyone else's life. But like it or not, it was now out in the open. And neither one of them knew what to do about it.

On the way home they had both been pretty quiet. Each one thinking their own thoughts. They stopped at the same gas station going back as they had on their way up. Both she and Seth had wanted a snack so she got out of the car to get it while Seth filled the car with gas. The moment she walked through the door, she realized her mistake. On the rack beside her were the t-shirts she had looked at before and couldn't make up her mind which one to get and ended up not getting either one. As she looked at them, she remembered the young man who had been standing beside her. She had left, but maybe he had stayed and bought the two t-shirts they found on their door at the lodge. She wondered if he was the same young man courting Sandy at the lodge. What were the chances of that happening?

Chloe turned around and left deciding she didn't really need a snack after all. Seth asked her to pick him up a snack, too, but she knew he would understand. So she was surprised when he yelled at her. She went and got in the pickup. Hurt, mad, angry? She didn't know which. After going into the store to get his snack, he got in the pickup and pulled out onto the highway. He was sorry for his outburst, but the words had already been spoken.

"Chloe, I'm sorry."

111

"It's fine. Don't worry about it. We are both under a lot of stress right now. It seems as if we have no control over our lives and it is very upsetting." But Chloe didn't forget.

Seth drove in silence. He was sorry for the things he had said, but he was so fed up. He decided it was once again time to touch base with Detective Bonner.

Later on that night Seth pulled into the garage. It had been a long trip. One that was met with silence the majority of the way home. Physically the trip wasn't so long, but mentally it had seemed as if it had lasted forever. With the garage door closing behind the pickup, they were both glad to be home.

"Do you want to take our stuff out now or tomorrow?"

"It's not that late. Why don't we get it out of the pickup now. If that's okay with you?"

"Sure, if you'll open the door, I'll grab the suitcases." Seth opened the back door of the pickup while Chloe opened the door into the house. Stepping through the door into the house she knew someone had been in the house while they were gone. She stood quietly trying to decide what made her feel that way. Seth was walking toward her with the suitcases, but she was standing in his way.

"Chloe. Move. Why are you standing in the way?"

"Someone has been here. I don't know how I know, but I know."

"How can you tell? You're not even in the house yet."

"I can feel it," Chloe said, slowly walking through the door and stopping on the other side.

"Well, I don't feel anything!" Seth said, as he marched through the house going to the bedroom and sitting the suitcases on the floor. He knew Chloe's intuition was good, but he didn't see, feel, or smell anything that would make him think someone had been in the house.

Seth sat the suitcases down just inside their bedroom door. "Chloe do you want to unpack now or in the.........?" Seth stopped speaking. On the bed, spread out on the comforter was the same t-shirt that was on the door to their room at the lodge.

"Why did you stop talking, Seth? I thought we might unpack in the morning. Maybe just sit and have some hot chocolate now. Maybe a little T.V. How does that sound?"

Chloe stopped talking when she got to their bedroom door. Seth was quiet and he was staring at the bed. "What is wrong with you?" Chloe's face turn white as her eyes followed Seth's in the direction of the bed.

"No, oh, no! No! No! No!" Chloe cried, falling to her knees right where she was standing.

———

The man stood watching the bedroom window. He had planned everything carefully. From spreading the t-shirt from Oklahoma out carefully on the bed, to placing a red rose in the middle and then the coup de gras was opening the curtains in the room. He wanted to make sure there was no mistake as to who it was from. If possible, he also wanted to see the look on their faces.

He smiled. He was glad he thought of that one small thing. It was so much better to watch her reaction than it was just to imagine it. The bonus was, he didn't just get to watch Chloe's, but he got to watch Seth's also. It couldn't get much better than that.

The man left as soon as they noticed the curtains were open and shut them. For the moment, there wasn't any reason for him to stay. He had accomplished what he had set out to do.

CHAPTER 18

"How did he beat us home, Seth?" Chloe asked, as Seth picked up the phone to call Detective Bonner's cell phone. He and Chloe had not slept well the night before and now they were up bright and early the next morning.

"I don't know, Chloe. Unless he wasn't in Oklahoma. But then there's the t-shirt on the door and they are the same t-shirts as the ones we just found on the bed. Then there is the rose on the shirt. Nothing fits."

Detective Bonner's cell phone went to voice mail so Seth decided to leave a message. After leaving the message, Seth turned toward Chloe. "It is so good to be home."

"Would you like some breakfast?" Chloe asked, looking in Seth's direction.

"I don't think so. Maybe later."

"Just coffee then."

"Yes, I guess so."

"It'll be ready in just a minute. Do you want to sit out on the patio?"

"I don't think so. I don't know. Yes, lets. If you'll hold off, I'll blow the patio off, clean the table and put the cushions on the chairs. It won't take me but a couple of minutes."

"Do you want me to help?"

"No, I've got it. Although I am rethinking breakfast. How about an egg sandwich with the coffee."

"Would you like some bacon on that egg sandwich?"

"Yes, this sandwich keeps getting better and better." Seth smiled at Chloe, then went to take care of the patio while she began working on the sandwiches.

"Do you think he's out there, Chloe?" Seth asked his wife once they were seated.

"I don't know. How can he be here when we left him in Oklahoma. Or so we thought? What do we do now?"

"What do we always do when we are facing something out of our control? We pray. If he is watching, and I hope he is, I want him to see us come together in prayer. He may not believe in prayer or in God, but we do."

Silence reigned for the moment as Chloe and Seth pulled their chairs together. Sitting across from each other they took hold of each other's hands and bowed their heads.

"Well, Lord, we're back. Once again our lives are completely out of control and fear is starting to make itself known. We need Your help. So as we come together, we are asking You for Your help. We don't know what to do. We ask for Your guidance. You know what is going on so we ask You to prepare the way before us and to help us make wise decisions..." Seth was cut short by the ringing of his cell phone. Just before he picked it up, he said a quick "Amen."

"Hello, Bob. I am so glad you returned my call. Chloe and I need to sit down and talk to you if that is okay."

"Seth, is this about the stalking?"

"Yes, I hate to say it, but yes it is."

"Why don't you and Chloe come to the house tonight for hamburgers. I know Julie would love to see Chloe and this way we can relax and talk things over."

"That sounds great. What time do you want us there?"

"Around six."

"Okay, we'll see you then." Detective Bonner said, as he hung up. He immediately picked up the phone to call his wife to see what they needed to do before the Kelley's got there. Since Julie had gone to the grocery store that day, she already had everything they would need.

Seth looked at Chloe as he told her they were going to the Bonner's house for supper.

"We probably should get all our thoughts down on paper before we go. That way we won't forget anything. As each memory pops into our mind, we can write it down. At least then we will be prepared."

"You know, Seth. I am getting really tired of living like this. Maybe we should just move and hope he doesn't follow us."

The man stood beside the tree within listening distance of Seth and Chloe's conversation. At least he could hear most of what was being said, and he didn't like it at all. Not at all. Somewhere during the time he had been stalking Chloe, he had decided he no longer wanted to kill her. He hadn't thought much beyond that.

"No way, Chloe! No way! You and I are destined to be together."

117

Seth and Chloe arrived at the detectives house a few minutes after six. At the last minute, they decided to stop and pick up some potato salad. Chloe had been uptight and did not want to fix anything. They decided to take the easy way out and stop at Wal-Mart.

Just as they turned into the driveway the Bonner's came from around the side of the house to meet them.

"Hi, Chloe. It's so nice to see you." Julie gave her friend a hug. "You're going to have to tell me all about your trip."

Detective Bonner stepped forward shaking Seth's hand and at the same time led him in the direction of the gate to the backyard.

"I thought we might talk for a little while before we put the hamburgers on. Does that suit you?"

"Yes, it does. There's a whole lot I would like to get off of my chest."

"Chloe, would it be alright with you if we sit over in the alcove?" Julie said looking at her friend. "I thought maybe we could talk while the guys talked. You always liked the alcove so I thought we could talk there."

"I don't mind at all Julie. In fact, I think I prefer it that way. It's easier to talk one on one to another woman than to talk to a man. Seth and I have been discussing this subject all day trying to make sure we had the information Bob needs."

Detective Bonner and Seth sat in the chairs on the patio. Chloe and Julie walked to their little alcove and sat down. This was Chloe's favorite place to sit in Julie's backyard. It was so peaceful. It had been carved out of some bushes just big enough to hold a bench. Because it was enclosed it gave Chloe a feeling of security.

Being enclosed, the bushes may have given Chloe and Julie a sense of security, but it gave the man in the bushes the opportunity to get close enough to them in order to hear them talking.

He smiled to himself as he listened to Chloe relate all that had been happening to her. He was very pleased. Things were definitely going his way.

After Chloe had told Julie about what had happened in Broken Bow, and then relayed what had just happened at their home when they got back, she was finally able to slow down and enjoy Julie's company. Julie had asked all the pertinent questions as they continued to sit and talk in the alcove. She and her husband had discussed Seth and Chloe's predicament and wanted to get Chloe's thoughts while Seth was not around. Julie had also memorized the questions Bob had wanted her to insert wherever she could. Not only did he want her to remember Chloe's answer to the question, but he wanted her to remember Chloe's reaction to the question and her demeanor when she heard and then answered it.

Chloe was her best friend and she was going to do everything in her power to help her. So she listened very intently to every word Chloe said knowing that Chloe's very life may depend on what she heard or saw.

Detective Bonner and Seth sat on the patio drinking coffee while they talked. In the beginning they were very relaxed, but when Bob directed the conversation toward what had happened in Oklahoma, Seth became very upset. The longer they talked, the more Seth's demeanor changed. He was uptight, angry, defensive, and exhausted.

Detective Bonner watched carefully as he and Seth continued to talk. What was going on with his friend's life. He didn't know, but he knew something wasn't feeling right to him. He always had a gut instinct that would lead him in one direction or another and now something was telling him something was not right.

The man couldn't hear what the men were saying. He was too far away from them. He watched their faces as he listened to Chloe and Julie talk.

Overall the man was satisfied with his night's excursion so he silently slipped off into the night. But before he had gone very far, he accidently stepped on a dried tree branch making quite a bit of noise.

"Darn," the man said out loud, as he stopped and stood very still.

"Julie, did you hear that?"

"Bob, could you come here for a minute?"

Detective Bonner knew that his wife would not have called him if wasn't important so he got up and headed toward the alcove. "What's up Julie?"

"Chloe and I both heard what sounded like someone stepping on a dry tree branch. Could you check it out please? Maybe Chloe's situation is making us paranoid or someone was out there listening."

Just then they all heard footsteps running away from the alcove.

"Go in the house Julie and take Chloe and Seth with you. Detective Bonner grabbed the gun that he kept with him at all times and headed out into the darkness of the woods.

"What is going on?" Seth asked Chloe and Julie. "Where is Bob going?"

"You need to come with us Seth. Chloe and I both heard something and Bob has gone to check it out. He told us to go in the house."

"Should I go help?"

"No, I think you would just be in the way. Plus you don't have a gun. Bob will call you if he needs you."

All three marched into the house shutting and locking the door behind them. No one felt like talking so they just stood there in silence as they waited for Detective Bonner to return. The silence surrounded them until they heard a gunshot. Again they waited for the detective to return, but he didn't.

Time passed until finally Seth said, "I either need to go check on Bob or we need to call the police. Just then several police cars pulled up in front of the house. Julie went out to meet them and to show them the direction that Bob had gone. Many of them had been there before so they were not unfamiliar with the area and began to run toward the woods.

———

Detective Bonner stood quietly listening. He knew someone was there, but he couldn't tell where. He had called for backup as soon as he realized there was someone there. And now, even though they were searching for him, he remained silent. He didn't want to give his position away. Gun in hand. Pointed toward the ground for safety. He remained still hoping whoever it was would make a mistake. His fellow officers continued coming in his direction. If he didn't want to get shot, he needed to let them know where he was.

After breaking his silence, he explained to the police officers what was going on. He would follow up with a written report tomorrow after he went to work. The police left and Julie turned toward her husband and their friends.

"Would anybody like some pizza?" Julie asked. "I think it's too late to start the hamburgers. Don't you?"

"I don't think anyone is in the mood to eat." Seth said. "Why don't we just go on home and come back another night?"

Detective Bonner and Julie stood there watching as Seth and Chloe drove away. "What was going on with Seth?" The detective asked himself, as he watched the tail lights of Kelley's car get smaller and smaller.

It had been a long night and Julie wanted to make sure the kitchen was clean before they went to bed. She looked around and since there wasn't anything for her to do, she walked over to the patio door staring into the darkness of the woods beyond. As she stared in the direction of the woods, she replayed the events of the night in her head. She went to turn the outside lights off and that is when she realized Bob was sitting on the patio.

"Bob, what are you doing out here?" Julie asked opening the door and walking toward where her husband was sitting.

"I was just sitting here thinking about all the events that took place this evening. Were you and Chloe able to have a good talk?"

"I suppose you can say we did. It was going really well there for a while."

"How was Chloe's demeanor? Does she seem to be holding up okay?" Detective Bonner asked, as he continued to sit in his chair with his feet propped up on the table in front of him and his fingers interlocked behind his neck staring into the darkness beyond.

"You know, Julie. I never really thought about what was happening to Chloe until tonight. It hit closer to home because you were sitting right beside her."

"I knew something was bothering you. The moment I came out here I realized you were sitting in your favorite position. The one that tells everyone to leave you alone. So what's going on?"

"To tell you the truth. I don't know." He stood up and took hold of Julie's hand. "I can't even imagine what the both of them are going through." He let Julie walk through the door in front of him. When he walked through the door, he pulled it shut and locked it.

"Come on. Let's get ready for bed. I don't know about you, but I am really tired."

"You've got a deal." Julie said, as she let her husband lead her toward the bedroom.

Detective Bonner got up early the next morning and left for the office without waking Julie. He had sat at the kitchen table jotting down some notes before he left the house knowing he could make whatever adjustments he needed to after he arrived at the office.

CHAPTER 19

With Summer gone and Fall halfway through, the nights had started lasting longer and getting cooler. The end of October was already here. Halloween was tomorrow night and Detective Bonner didn't like it. He had never liked Halloween as a kid, he didn't like it as an adult, and he really didn't like it as part of the police force. People did stupid things on Halloween. Really stupid things. Adults and kids alike were full of mischief. Kids he could give a little slack, but adults, they should know better.

Detective Bonner sat at his desk. Tomorrow night everyone would have to work. The chief wanted their presence known, hoping it would cut down on the vandalism and the pranks. He was supposed to have the day off, but it was cancelled which is probably why he was a little testy with everyone today.

As he sat at his desk, his thoughts drifted off to Chloe. She and Julie were enjoying their self-defense classes. The stalker seemed to have taken a sabbatical. He didn't know if this man had gone underground for a while, or if he had just decided to leave town. He didn't really care what he had done. He just hoped he was no longer interested in Chloe.

"Detective Bonner, I believe this is for you. I found it on my desk. I'm sorry, but I don't know how long it has been there."

Detective Chin said, as he handed the envelope to Detective Bonner.

The detective took the envelope and started to open it, but noticed it did not have a stamp on it. "Thanks, Chin. I appreciate it." He said, immediately walking off in the direction of the forensics lab.

As he entered the lab, Detective Bonner spoke to the technician that was there.

"Dave, can you do me a favor?"

"I'm a little busy right this minute, Bob. Does it have to be right now?"

"Yes, Dave. It needs to be right now." Detective Bonner then explained the reasoning behind his request.

"It may be nothing. I just want to know if there are any prints at all."

After Dave dusted the envelope for fingerprints, he handed the paper back to Detective Bonner.

"Sorry, Bob."

"I really didn't think there would be. Let me read what's inside. Then if you would, maybe you could just see if there are any fingerprints on the letter. If there are, then we will decide what to do." He pulled the paper out of the envelope and began to read.

"She's Mine. She belongs to Me." The note was written in very large letters.

"What does it say, Bob?"

"Read it for yourself, Dave. Would you dust it before you read it? I keep hoping he will make a mistake, but so far he hasn't."

"He still hasn't. I can't find anything on either one."

"I wish he had sealed the envelope then maybe we would have had a chance at some DNA, but we lost out there, too." Detective Bonner said, as he turned around and went back to his desk.

Halloween night arrived and all hands were on deck. Police cars were out in full force. They were making themselves known in hopes of cutting down on the mischief Halloween night seemed to bring out in people of all ages.

The man watched the trick-or-treaters go from house to house. He loved Halloween. He liked the costumes and the more gruesome the better. He was in his element.

"Trick-or-Treat!" The kids were saying as they went from house to house. He knew he didn't want the treat; he wanted the trick. He loved the tricks played on others at Halloween. Actually, he wanted to be the one to do a big trick. Something with a bang to it. That always went over quite well with the police.

The call came in at 7:50p.m. The girl who answered the phone was a college kid. She was working in Customer Service so she could make extra money for Christmas. So when the phone rang, she was the one who answered. She listened intently to what was being said. By the time the person on the phone was finished speaking, the girl was shaking so hard she almost dropped the phone on the counter. She tried hard to remember the code red word for today, but she couldn't. She was so scared she couldn't even think. So all she could do was repeat the call for the manager over the P.A.

The manager walked over to the counter. He had been close by when he heard her call. At his arrival, the co-ed told him what the person on the phone said, he turned white, looked at the clock, which now showed 7:55p.m., and decided to empty the store while at the same time calling 911.

The man watched as the manager took the microphone from the girl's hand so he could make the announcement for all the customers to exit the store. At that moment he knew it was his clue to leave the store himself. He handed a note to a young boy telling him to give it to his mother who was standing just a few feet away. On the front of the note was one word. POLICE.

As the electronics door opened at the front of the store and the man walked out, the manager's voice came over the sound system. "May I have your attention please!" He waited, then once again tried to speak calmly into the stores sound system. "May I have your attention? Please!" At the same moment he began to speak, his mind was racing trying to think of something he could say, anything, that would get the customers to leave the store immediately.

He remembered a situation that had been in the news a few days before about two women having a fight in the bleach aisle of some grocery store somewhere around Houston. The fumes had caused several people to become sick. So the manager decided to use this as a way to get people to leave the store.

"Would everyone please exit through the front of the store. There has been a chemical spill at the back of the store and the fumes could be harmful. Thank you for exiting the store as soon as possible!!!!"

He turned to the girl to see if she had called the police. She had so they both made their way to the front of the store to await their arrival.

It was now 7:57p.m. Everyone had been very compliant and had listened to the announcement leaving the store as fast as they could without scaring the kids.

The police station was a short distance away so it did not take them long to get there. They pulled up in front of the store and when one of the officers got out of his car, and asked a large group of people who the manager was. Ken Johnson stepped forward to explain what had happened and just as he did a woman ran over and handed the police officer an envelope. He opened it and on the piece of paper inside was one word. KABOOM!!!!!!

CHAPTER 20

Last night's escapade by someone had ticked off the whole police department. Most of them had had their wives, children, and friends at Wal-Mart when it happened. Julie and the kids had been there. Worst of all, they had been there during the so called prank. If it was a prank, it wasn't funny.

Detective Bonner was sitting at his desk. He was sitting in his favorite position. He was just as frustrated as everyone else and he needed time to concentrate. From out of the corner of his eye, he saw one of the police officers approaching. He came over and put an envelope in front of him.

"I think this may belong to you."

"What makes you think so?"

"Well, one of the guys mentioned you had received an envelope yesterday with a message inside. A young boy was given this one in the store last night addressed to the police. I thought maybe you could compare the two of them and see if they could be matched in any way."

Detective Bonner pulled his desk drawer open and picked up the envelope he had been given the day before. He took the one from the officer and laid them side by side as he compared them.

"They look the same to me."

"Yes. I think they do, too. So if you want them, they're yours."

"Thanks. I don't know how they relate, but I am sure hoping that they do."

Detective Bonner continued to sit at his desk. He pushed his chair back getting in his favorite concentrating position. This way he knew no one would bother him. This time he was actually trying to put the two envelopes together, instead of trying to get his heart to calm down. Julie and the kids had been at Wal-Mart last night. Worst of all they had been there when the hoax was taking place. Thankfully it was a hoax. But what if it hadn't been?

When the call had come in to the station from the co-ed, the heart of everyone on that call had dropped to the bottom. What did this man think he was doing? Was this Chloe's stalker? How did he find him? How did he connect them? He had nothing to go on. So now he replayed in his mind what had taken place last night.

When he, Detective Roberts and Detective Chin had pulled up behind the police car last night, he had seen Julie and the kids standing off to the side. He walked up to one of the police officers standing in front of Wal-Mart, while at the same time motioning Julie to come to him. The officer began to tell him what had taken place.

Detective Bonner listened and when the officer was finished, he pulled Julie off to the side.

"Julie, thank God you and the kids are safe."

As he held them for just a moment in time, he said a quick prayer to the only one who could help him. "Lord, God. I really need Your help. I think this is Chloe's stalker. I think he is getting more frustrated. I don't know for sure. It's only a gut feeling. But the one thing I do know is I need Your help. I'm pretty sure if we solve Chloe's case, we'll also solve this one. Thank you, for taking care of my family. Amen."

As he stared at the envelopes in front of him, he couldn't get the Kelley's out of his mind. Now that Chloe and Julie were taking self-defense classes together their friendship had deepened. The classes helped. They always did something together before or after their class. He now had more of an appreciation for what the Kelley's were going through than he had before. For when evil is on your doorstep, you have a different perspective to what is happening.

Detective Bonner continued praying as he sat in his chair making it clear to everyone he didn't want to be disturbed. "Father, we have nothing to go on. I ask You to go before us and prepare the way. I thank You, Lord, for what You are doing, for what You have done, and for what You are about to do. Amen."

———

While Detective Bonner was sitting at his desk praying, the man was back. He was standing beside the tree in the woods behind Chloe's house. He had enjoyed himself immensely last night. He had been able to walk around among all the people without being detected.

He had been able to enjoy himself from the beginning to the end. He didn't know if the police considered what he had done last night as a hoax, or if they had actually connected it to Chloe's case. He didn't know, but he didn't care. Now it was time to get down to business once again.

CHAPTER 21

He had never taken this long with a victim before, but this victim kept leaving. Where she went, he didn't know. But, he was persistent and he certainly didn't give up with minor setbacks. Today had been one of his persistent days. Periodically, he would stop by the Kelley's house just to see if they were back from wherever it was they had gone. And today, his persistence had paid off. She was there.

Chloe and Seth had been home for over a couple of months now. Seth had gone on another troubleshooting job for his company and had taken Chloe with him. And now they were playing catch up on getting their swimming pool and yard ready for spring time.

It had taken Seth all morning, but he had finally finished mowing the yard. Chloe had been out picking up sticks and making sure there wasn't anything in the way of the mower. Once that was done, she set about getting the front yard decorated. She wanted to move to the backyard, but she was leery. She was afraid. She didn't know how she was going to feel about being there, but she had done all she could do in the front yard. It was getting close to lunch time and she wanted to have lunch on the patio. She could see Seth had just about finished with all the mowing. It was time to face her fear.

Chloe gathered up all her tools, putting them in her gardening wagon. Then she pulled the wagon around to the back patio. She stopped close to, but not on the cement. She dropped the handle then headed toward the garage. She wanted to blow the patio off before she fixed sandwiches for herself and Seth.

Chloe returned to the patio with the blower. After plugging it in, she watched as the leaves swirled in circles finally making their way off of the patio. Back and forth she went. She had only been working a few minutes when she felt his presence. He must be really close because she felt sick to her stomach. She didn't want to let him know she knew he was there, but she couldn't think of anything she could do. If she could just finish blowing off the patio, she could go in the house without alerting him to the fact she knew he was there. She looked up just as Seth came around the corner of the house.

"Let's go in and eat. I am starving."

Chloe turned off the blower while at the same time thanking God for allowing her to be able to leave the patio without letting the man know she was aware of his presence. When she reached her hand for the door handle, Seth could see how bad her hand was shaking.

"He's out there. Isn't he, Chloe?" Seth asked, as he followed her through the patio door.

"I think so. No, I know so! What are we supposed to do, Seth? This man, whoever he is, is destroying our lives."

"Are we going to let him destroy us, Chloe, or are we going to fight?"

"I'm scared, Seth. I am so tired of being afraid. I'm afraid of what this is doing to our marriage. I am just tired. I hate thinking this, but I keep wondering where God is. We have prayed so many times, but I don't see anything happening. So where is He, Seth? Where is He?"

"I don't know, Chloe. But I do know He is working on our behalf. I know I don't have to remind you, but the Bible says *'He will never leave, nor forsake us.'* So I guess we'll just have to stand on that promise. If you'll fix us some lunch, I'm going to call Detective Bonner."

"Okay!" Chloe said, as she stood by the sink, tears filling her eyes. She went to the refrigerator and pulled out everything she needed for sandwiches. She stood in front of the window periodically looking out into the darkness of the woods behind their house. She had put lace curtains on the windows quite a while back. It gave her the ability to see out, but no one could see in.

After finishing the sandwiches, Chloe put them on the table then went into the pantry to get some chips.

"Seth, lunch is ready." Chloe said, while in the process of sitting everything on the table.

"I'll be there in just a minute. I'm talking to Detective Bonner."

"Do you want me to send someone out to look around?" Detective Bonner asked.

"To tell you the truth, Bob, I don't know. We live so far out and if he knew you were on your way, he would have plenty of time to leave."

"Well, Seth. You're in luck. I had to go to Woodville this morning and I am on my way back to Livingston. I am just a couple of minutes from your turnoff. I can be there in about ten minutes."

"That's great. Thanks, Bob. I really appreciate it." Seth hung up and went back into the kitchen.

"Chloe, why don't you fix an extra sandwich? Detective Bonner will be here in a few minutes." Seth said, as he told Chloe about his conversation with the detective.

After making an extra sandwich, and sitting it on the table with the other two, Seth and Chloe walked through the door to the garage and pushed the garage door opener at the same time. They were standing in front of the garage when Detective Bonner pulled up and stopped right in front of them.

"I hear we have a problem on our hands."

"You could say that." Seth said, walking up to Detective Bonner and shaking his hand.

"Would you like to eat lunch with us, Bob?" Chloe asked, as they entered the kitchen.

"Yes, that would be nice. Would it be possible to eat on the patio? It may sound silly, but I would like to see if I can feel what you feel."

"That's fine, Detective. If you and Seth will go outside and sit down, I'll bring the sandwiches out."

"Chloe, we can help."

"No, Seth. If you and Bob will go outside, he will have a few minutes to relax. If you know what I mean?"

"Yes, I do. Good thinking, Chloe."

Seth and Detective Bonner went outside and sat down. Chloe followed with a wet rag so she could clean off the table. Then she turned around and went back inside.

Chloe already had the sandwiches made so she made some tea. In about five minutes she took the tea outside, put it on the table, then she turned around and went back to get the sandwiches.

While Seth and the detective waited on Chloe, they talked quietly. Not about anything in particular for the detective was trying to feel the man's presence.

While sitting the glasses on the table, Chloe turned to Detective Bonner and asked, "Okay, Bob, can you feel anything?" The detective didn't answer.

"Bob, did you feel anything?"

No answer

"Bob, did you feel anything?" Chloe asked, as she spoke each word slowly and directly at the detective.

"Yes, Chloe. I did. Now I need both, you and Seth to go in the house right this minute. I am going into the woods to look around. Both of you, stay here!"

"I am not letting you go into the woods by yourself, Bob. It's not going to happen."

"Seth listen to me. I need you to stay with Chloe. Now do what I said."

Seth and Chloe stood and went into the house while at the same time, Detective Bonner stood and headed in the direction of the woods.

After several minutes, Seth and Chloe heard a gunshot. Being surprised by the sound they both were paralyzed not knowing what they should do.

"Chloe, you know I have to go check on Bob. Go in the house and wait until I get back."

"Not on your life Seth. You are not leaving me here by myself."

Seth grabbed his gun from the gun cabinet and they both headed for the patio door. They stopped and said a quick prayer then headed towards the woods. They ran in the same direction the detective had taken. When they reached the edge of the woods they slowed down, not sure what they were going to find. Progress was slow because they didn't know if the man was still there or not. Seth put his hand out to stop Chloe. As they stood there, he could feel what Chloe had been telling him all along.

They continued to stand still. Something told Seth to be quiet and not to move. It was then they heard Bob moan. They moved in the direction of the sound. Once again Seth said a quick prayer, "Oh' Lord! We could sure use some help right now."

Slowly they pressed forward moving branches and bushes out of their way. They stopped for their lying on the ground right in front of them, was Bob. He was still. Very still.

CHAPTER 22

The man had been watching Chloe all morning while she and her husband worked around the house. He watched as Seth cleaned in and around the pool. That made him very happy for it could only mean one thing. Chloe was going to start swimming again. He was looking forward to that. He watched Chloe go before Seth picking up anything that could get in the way of the mower. After getting a lot of big branches out of the way, she started decorating, leaving the mowing to Seth. It took a while, but once she had finished what she thought needed to be done, she picked up her tools and put them in a wagon and headed to the back of the house.

From his vantage point, he could see the backyard better than any other part of the yard including the swimming pool area, although, the pool was a close second. He watched as she went around the edge of the house returning immediately with the blower. She plugged it in and began to blow off all the leaves and dirt that had gathered on the patio. She was half-way through when Seth came around the edge of the house. From small catches in their conversation, he could tell they were going in to eat lunch. Which would probably take at least an hour. Since it was such a nice day, he didn't know if they would eat outside or not.

The man waited several minutes then walked over to the pool. He put his hand in the water. It was cool. He knew it would probably be several days before Chloe actually began swimming. He loved watching Chloe swim. He stood for just a minute enjoying the smell of freshly mown grass and the smell of the flowers Chloe had put around the pool. All at once he decided to return to his favorite spot. He didn't know if Seth and Chloe had finished eating or not, but figured he would hang around long enough to see if they were going to come back out or not. If they didn't, he would leave and return tomorrow.

Returning to his favorite spot, he made sure the branches and leaves covered him completely. He settled in, and that's when he heard a car pull up in the driveway. He heard the mumbled greetings as whoever it was who came to visit entered the garage at the same time the Kelley's did. He berated himself because he had settled in too soon and did not know who had come to visit. If the timing had been different, whoever was there right now could have seen him as he stood by the pool. He let his guard down for one moment and now look what had happened.

———

Detective Bonner pulled up in front of the Kelley's house and as he did, his eyes searched his surroundings, starting with the area where the pool was located. He thought he might have seen Seth by the pool, but then Seth and Chloe walked out to welcome him. Did he, or did he not see someone by the pool. It had been only a shadow so he wasn't sure.

"Are you hungry, Bob? Would you like a sandwich?" Chloe asked. She had made an extra sandwich knowing the detective was on his way. Chloe knew Seth wouldn't eat if the detective didn't. Detective Bonner saw both Seth and Chloe's surprised looks when he asked if it would be alright if they could eat outside. He smiled at Chloe as she did a double take when he said he wanted to see if he could feel what she felt when she knew the man was there.

"Intuition! Intuition is the word I think you're looking for, Detective." Chloe said, smiling at the detectives struggle for the right word. "Using your intuition sounds a lot better than seeing if you can feel anything." When Chloe finished talking, they all went outside.

Detective Bonner knew Chloe was scared, but he needed them to be outside. As he watched Chloe wipe off the table, his senses were on high alert. He wanted to catch this guy really bad. Not only was he threatening Chloe, he was threatening an entire town. You never knew what he was going to do. Halloween had been an example of that.

Seth and the detective sat there quietly talking while Chloe went back into the house to get the sandwiches. After Chloe had finished putting everything on the table, she sat down, too. No one wanted to sit with their backs to the woods, so each one made sure their chairs faced each other and the woods at the same time. As Detective Bonner sat there, he realized something. It was as if a light bulb had gone off in his head. He jumped to his feet and told Seth and Chloe to go in the house while at the same time he pulled out his gun. As he headed toward the woods, his pace slowed his eyes continually on the move.

"Where are you guys? I can't wait. Follow when you get here." The detective said, as he spoke into his shoulder radio.

Detective Bonner was a cautious man. As he went deeper into the woods, he changed his method of searching. He slowed to a walk, checking every bush and tree along the way. He came to the clearing and stopped. Not sure whether he wanted to cross the clearing or not, he stood for a moment just listening to the sounds around him. He knew if he did, he would be exposed.

What seemed like a very long time was actually only a few minutes. Making the decision, he acted quickly. Not wanting to be exposed any longer than necessary, Detective Bonner sat out at a dead run across the clearing. The clearing wasn't very large and he had hoped he could make it to the other side. He couldn't. A shot rang out and the detective fell to the ground.

The man stood watching and he knew the exact moment when the detective figured out his secret. So instead of running when the detective headed his way, he stayed right where he was. He watched as the detective approached. He smiled while waiting for him to make up his mind whether he was going to cross the clearing or not. By this time the man knew Detective Bonner well enough to know he would. It was just a matter of time. He just had to watch and wait.

The moment Detective Bonner left the safety of the woods, the man was ready. He quickly took aim and fired. He watched as the detective fell to the ground. He headed toward the detective to make sure he was dead, but he could hear someone coming. He quickly decided it was time for him to leave.

Seth and Chloe made their way to Detective Bonner's side.

"Seth, there's so much blood. What do we do?" Chloe asked, as they both fell to their knees beside the detective.

Seth had seen his friend speak into his radio before. He thought he saw him speak into the mic just before he entered the woods. He wasn't sure, but he hoped so. For if he had, he knew the police were already on their way. Seth reached down and picked the mic up from beside his friend's body, and spoke to it, "Officer down! I repeat! Officer down!"

"Chloe, let me have your jacket. Maybe I can stop some of the bleeding while we're waiting for them to get here." Seth reached for Chloe's jacket after taking off his own. He placed Chloe's jacket under the detectives head. Then he placed his jacket on top of the detective and spread it out hoping to bring some warmth to his body. After getting both of the jackets in place, he applied pressure to the area of the detective's wound.

"Chloe, you need to run up to the house so you can show the police how to get here."

Chloe stood for just a moment with fear and indecision clearly at war on her face. But then she took a deep breath and ran in the direction of the house. A shot rang out and Chloe fell to the ground.

The man was glad he had delayed his departure. He couldn't have planned things any better than what had just taken place. Now it really was time for him to go. He set off at a dead run for his motorcycle.

Seth had his hands full and could not follow.

"Chloe, are you alright?" Seth asked. He was trying to decide whether to let go of the detective's wound or not. He knew if he did, he might die.

"Oh, God, Chloe. Answer me. Are you alright?" He repeated, staring at the blood coming from under Chloe's body. Just as Seth made the decision to let go of the detective to go to Chloe, she groaned and moved a little bit. Then she slowly sat up.

"Chloe, stay where you are! Don't get up. Lay back down."

Hearing the sounds of the police arriving at the house, Seth once again pushed the button on the detective's radio and told them where to find them. Letting them know Chloe had been shot, too. As the police got to the edge of the clearing, Seth could hear the ambulance arrive at the house. Thankful that the police had arrived and the paramedics were not far behind, he let one of the policemen take over for him so he could go to Chloe.

The paramedics arrived bringing one stretcher. They went directly to Detective Bonner after having been advised Chloe's wound was not life threatening. The paramedics quickly checked the detective over before putting him on the stretcher. The detective laid there. Very quiet and very still.

The paramedics navigated the terrain of the woods as fast as they could. After arriving back at the ambulance and putting the detective inside, they took off with lights and sirens going. When the ambulance carrying Detective Bonner drove away, another ambulance arrived. This one would be for Chloe. The paramedics checked her over a little more thoroughly now that the detective was on his way. Knowing that her wound wasn't life threatening, it was still necessary that she go to the hospital. So they put her on a stretcher and navigated the same terrain the previous paramedics had gone through to get Detective Bonner to his ambulance. Not knowing exactly what the situation entailed two ambulances had been sent to the Kelley's house.

Knowing that Chloe was going to be okay, Seth decided to follow in his car. He bent over and gave Chloe a kiss, noticing how pale she was. She tried to give him a smile, but failed to do so.

The paramedics placed Chloe in the back of the ambulance while Seth went to get in his car, which was still in the garage. He sat there and waited. It seemed as if it was taking an awfully long time for them to get going. Just as he decided to get out and check to see what was going on, the ambulance took off. As it left, Seth noticed both paramedics were still standing there.

CHAPTER 23

"**B**ack Off!!" The man said, glaring at the paramedic. "Back Off!! Now!!" Once again the man spoke as loud as he could to get his point across while at the same time not speaking loud enough to alert anyone to his presence. The man was glad he had made the snap decision to change his plans. He had decided to return to the side of the house near the barn while waiting for another opportunity to present itself. So far today, he was lucky in that regard.

He watched the first ambulance drive off. He must be hurt pretty bad because both the siren and the lights were going. He watched as the two paramedics got the stretcher out of the back of the other ambulance and head toward the woods leaving it unattended. He slipped from his hiding place and ran to get in the driver's side of the ambulance. Then he sat and waited for them to return.

When the paramedics returned, they placed Chloe in the back. When the driver approached his side of the ambulance, the man pointed his gun at him telling him to call his friend and to tell him he needed him for just a minute.

"Hey, Jerry. Come here. I need your help."

Instead of listening to his partner, Jerry approached the passenger's side of the ambulance. He tried to open the door, but it wouldn't open. He looked through to the driver's side and saw the man pointing a gun right at him.

"Come to this side of the ambulance. Do it and do it now! Don't make a sound and I might, just might, let you live."

Jerry moved slowly to Dave's side, as they both stared at the gun in the man's hand. In sync, they both moved away from the ambulance. They stood there in shock as they watched the man drive away in their ambulance.

Seth had been blocked in the garage by the ambulance and was now waiting for the ambulance to get out of his way. They had already put Chloe in the back and while he sat there watching, Jerry had walked to driver's side. He had wondered what was going on, but guessed they would take off pretty soon. And they did. The only problem was the paramedics weren't the one's that were in the driver's seat. For a moment Seth sat there stunned, what in the world was going on.

Backing out and then pulling up beside both men Seth asked, "What is going on?" While Jerry took off to tell the police what happened, Dave explained to Seth. Seth turned white as a ghost then he sped off down the driveway.

The police were just now returning to the house and had only made it to the edge of the woods when Jerry ran up to them telling them what just happened. Seth had already left in pursuit of the ambulance knowing he had to keep it in his sight or Chloe was going to be in a lot of trouble.

———

Chloe knew something wasn't quite right. The ambulance was leaving and she was in the back by herself. She was pretty sure someone was supposed to be in the back with her. She knew she had been shot. She knew she had lost a lot of blood. She knew one of the paramedics should be with her. So what was going on?

Chloe laid there in silence. Fear was threatening to overcome her. She didn't know what was going on, but she sure didn't like it. But before it had a chance to grab hold of her, a Bible verse came to mind. She knew it was found in II Timothy. But where in II Timothy, she could not remember. All she could remember were the words, *"For God hath not given us the spirit of fear; but of power and of love, and of a sound mind."*

"Okay, Lord. Right this minute I really, really need a sound mind. I can't think. I need Your help. I am consumed by fear. So I ask You now for Your help to overcome what seems to be overcoming me. Clear my mind so I can think. I am in so much trouble right now. Help me, Lord. Please."

As Chloe finished her short prayer, another verse immediately came to her mind. Romans 10:13 *"For whosoever shall call upon the name of the Lord, shall be saved."*

"Well, Lord, I am calling and I am calling as loud as I possibly can." At that very moment, the man lost control of the ambulance. It weaved from side to side on the road for a span of a few seconds, although it seemed like an eternity. Finally, it flipped over coming to a rest on its side in an open field bordering a bunch of trees.

The man got out of the driver's side of the ambulance and ran toward the back doors. He saw Seth's car getting closer. He looked further down the road and saw the police cars with their lights flashing. As he stood there, he could hear not only the sirens getting closer, but he could also see Seth's car come to a screeching halt. He knew Seth would not follow him because of

Chloe. So staring once more in the direction of the police cars, the man ran to the safety of the trees.

"Oh, God." Seth cried out. No other words came to his mind as he ran to the ambulance and started trying to open the doors. Chloe was in there and he couldn't get in to see if she was alright. The police and the second ambulance arrived at the same time. The second ambulance had been called when the first ambulance took off without paramedics. The second ambulance had headed in the direction of the Kelley's house waiting for directions as it drove. The coordinating could not have been better if it had been planned. When the driver of the first ambulance pulled up behind the driver of the second ambulance, he had a sinking feeling. In the roll over, the doors had been crushed enough so they would not open. Both of the paramedics rushed to the back of the first ambulance.

Pushing Seth aside, the first paramedic to arrive told Seth, "I'm sorry, but get out of the way."

Then the police ran up to the ambulance and as they did, they asked the paramedics, "Is there any way we can help?"

———

Chloe laid there listening to the sounds being made on the outside of the ambulance. She heard Seth ask if they thought she was going to be okay. She knew he was scared for her because there was no way they could have known without being able to examine her. And they couldn't even get to her.

She could hear what she thought was probably a fire truck arrive. The activity around the ambulance picked up and she could hear what she believed to be the "jaws of life" coming to life. The sound not only filled her with joy, but scared her a little bit. What if they weren't able to get her out in time? So many what if's were running through her mind? She decided to leave it in God's hands as she drifted off into unconsciousness.

The ambulance had been crushed in a way where the doors were slightly open, but not open enough to be able to help the paramedics get to Chloe.

When Chloe returned to consciousness, she could feel the warmth on her shoulder. She knew she must be bleeding again. She also didn't know how long she had been unconscious. The ambulance rolling over hadn't helped her shoulder at all. As she laid there waiting for them to get to her, she wondered whether or not they had captured the man who had kidnapped her.

As Chloe listened, she heard a fireman place the jaws-of-life in what she assumed would be the best area to do the most good in opening the door. She heard the sound of metal on metal. The door started making a crunching screeching noise. Groaning as it ever so slowly began to give way. Finally, there was a loud pop and the one door separated itself from the other door, but not enough to be able to get Chloe out. The firemen pulled and tugged at the doors, but neither one would budge. After standing back and again assessing what needed to be done, the fireman holding the jaws-of-life saw a small opening on the side where the hinges were located. He placed the tip of the jaws-of-life as far in as it would go and began to listen to see if it made any difference. Once more the doors began to creak, screech and groan. Each time the fireman would make a little dent in the opening, he would push the tips further in. It was a slow process, but it was working. Those who were standing by watching were elated.

When the hole finally got big enough to where the fireman actually had some leverage, he stuck the jaws-of-life in as far as it would go and started putting some serious pressure on getting the doors open. Once again the machine began to make all sorts of horrible sounds, then with a final groan the door gave way. The fireman stood back, laid the jaws-of-life on the ground, and motioned for some help. When the door finally gave way it did so, so quickly that it made the firemen stumble and fall ending up in a pile outside the ambulance door. A shout of triumph came not only from the firemen on the ground, but from everyone watching. Most of all Seth.

With the ambulance now being accessible, one of the paramedics stepped forward to enter through the doors that were now open enough to allow entrance. As he approached Chloe, he saw her watching him.

"How are you doing, Chloe?" He asked, while at the same time noticing there was fresh blood on her shirt. He knew she was probably in shock, but she seemed to be doing far better than what he had expected.

"Dave, I need your help!" Jerry yelled. "This stretcher isn't going anywhere. I need to see if I can grab her under her arms and you need to see if you can grab her legs. I'm not sure how we are going to accomplish this, but we need to get going. You probably also need someone behind you to steady and guide you so you won't end up falling."

Jerry looked at Dave as he entered the opening behind him. "This is going to be a little tricky. She's got several minor cuts and bruises, but her main problem as far as I can tell, is still the gunshot wound. It's reopened and she's bleeding profusely. We need to get her out of here as fast as we can so we can take care of her shoulder. There just isn't enough room to do anything in here. And from the looks of it, she's going into shock. Let's get a move on it."

"Casey!" Dave yelled, picking Chloe up by her legs. Jerry and Dave had hitched a ride with one of the policeman after the man had taken off in their ambulance. They had arrived only seconds before the second ambulance. Casey and Jim were the paramedics in the second ambulance. Casey was right behind him and he heard all that Jerry said and was ready to do what was needed. His partner, Jim, was standing by with a new stretcher just out of the way so he would not get in the way with what they were trying to do.

Jerry had Chloe under her arms and slowly navigated through the stuff that had fallen on the floor during the roll over. He needed to move slowly. Not only because he didn't want the arm to start bleeding more than it already was, but he didn't want to cause her any more pain than was necessary.

Dave had Chloe's legs and both of them held her securely in their arms as they slowly inched their way toward the door. Casey was standing at Dave's back as he slowly made his way out of the door. He was ready to help anyway he could. All Dave had to do was to tell him what was needed.

When Chloe's legs came through the door, Jerry called out, "Casey, is there any way you can get Chloe's waist and work yourself up towards her arms then pull her out the best you can? There is so much stuff on the floor and what was on the sides seems to be coming down. I am not stable enough to hold on to her. I'm afraid I might fall."

While Jerry was talking, Jim, Casey's partner, ran to the other side of Chloe as she was slowly extracted from the ambulance. With Dave at her feet and Casey and Jim at her waist, they slowly began to pull her out of the ambulance. Two of the policemen got the stretcher and slowly navigated it into position so the paramedics were finally able to put Chloe on it. With Chloe safely on the stretcher, they all breathed a sigh of relief. As they found a spot where they could set the stretcher down safely, they heard a lot of commotion in the ambulance. Jerry had fallen and everyone could hear it.

After freeing himself from whatever had wrapped itself around his feet, Jerry jumped from the ambulance and landed safely on the ground not far from Chloe's stretcher. Since there was four of them, each paramedic took one corner of the stretcher then stood up walking as fast as they could to the waiting ambulance.

Once Chloe was placed safely inside, Casey got in beside her and made her as comfortable as he could. Jim started toward the driver's door of the ambulance while at the same time looking back toward Jerry and Dave. "Thanks a lot for your help. Would the two of you like to ride along?"

"No, I think we better stay with our ambulance. But thanks for the offer. It's appreciated."

"Where are you taking my wife?" Seth asked one of the paramedics.

"Lufkin Memorial." Jim said, driving away.

"Okay, I'm going to follow." Seth said.

While Chloe laid there listening to everything that was being said, her only thought was, "Thank You, Lord, for saving my life."

The ambulance sped off leaving everyone else behind.

CHAPTER 24

"**H**ow can you be so stupid, Clay? All I asked you to do was to watch. Watch and wait. That's all. Watch and wait. What was so hard about that?" The man asked, as he picked up a bottle that was close to him and threw it across the room hitting the wall. It hit and shattered into hundreds of little pieces.

"It was such an easy assignment." The man griped.

"I didn't say one thing about shooting anyone. Nothing. I said to watch and to wait." Once again the man picked up a bottle and threw it at the wall. "I can't believe you were so stupid. Get out! Get out before I ring your neck!" Looking at his brother, Clay decided the best thing to do at this point in time was to leave. Looking at his brother's face he decided the faster the better.

Slowly the man calmed down. Glancing around the room at the mess he made he tried to regain his composure. He had work to do.

Detective Bonner was out of surgery and in his private room at the hospital with a police officer stationed just outside his door. No one was to go in or out without being accompanied by that same police officer. Since the detective was still groggy from the surgery, the police officer had strict instructions to not let anyone in. And those that were let in, no matter who they were, were to be watched closely.

Chloe was also in her room. Once the doctors had looked at her arm, she too had a police officer stationed outside of her door. That officer had the same instructions as the other one.

It had been late into the night before both Chloe and Detective Bonner had made it to their rooms. It had taken Julie an hour and fifteen minutes to drive there and that was after she had taken the kids to her mothers. Julie and Seth sat in the waiting room talking to one another. There were long intervals of complete silence then when one or the other would think of something they would talk for a short while. Then once again, silence.

"I knew the stalking had started up again, but I didn't realize it had escalated from stalking to action." Julie said, as she looked over at him sitting in the chair in front of her.

"To tell you the truth, Julie, we didn't either. One minute we were sitting on the patio having sandwiches and tea and the next Bob had jumped up and headed for the woods. He must have figured something out, but I don't know what. It was as if a light bulb went off in his head."

"Julie, I am so sorry," Seth said with remorse.

"She's going to be alright Seth. They are both going to be alright," Julie said, as she stared at the waiting room wall.

Seth and Julie sat quietly in the same room. Each one thinking their own thoughts. They had each been told the surgeries had gone well, but had not reached the point where they could go be with their spouses.

Julie had a book on her lap, but so far had yet to read the first word. Seth had picked up a magazine, but it laid unopened on his lap. All was quiet. At least as quiet as a hospital can be. They had both decided that while they waited for Bob and Chloe to be put in their rooms, they would rather be with each other than by themselves. Even if they rarely spoke to each other, it was better not to be alone.

———

The man was frustrated. It had not taken much effort to find out which hospital Chloe had been taken to, but he couldn't find out any information on either one. He had gone to the ICU floor, but when he got out of the elevator and saw the two policemen that were standing guard over Detective Bonner and Chloe, he had to pretend he had gotten off on the wrong floor.

"I'm sorry, but evidently I am not on the maternity floor," the man had said to one of the nurses as they looked his way. They smiled at him and one of the nurses came forward and gave him directions. Once the officers heard him ask for the maternity floor, they turned back to the doors they were guarding unaware this was the man that had shot both Mrs. Kelley and Detective Bonner.

After receiving directions from the nurse, the man turned and got back into the elevator. He pushed the button for the main floor and on arriving he exited the hospital just as fast as he could. He returned to his car and drove off. He was so frustrated with the turn of events. It had seemed as if everything was going his way and then all of a sudden nothing was going his way.

The man pulled into the parking lot of the closest Jack-in-the Box. He wasn't that hungry, but he needed to sit somewhere. So he grabbed his computer and headed for the door. Once he entered, he saw the corner booth was not occupied so he placed his order and went to sit down. When his number was called, he picked it up, returned to the corner and sat down. He was ready. He needed to think.

The computer was a perfect guise. He ate his sandwich while pretending to be engrossed by something on his computer's screen. No one approached him. He sat there completely engrossed in trying to figure out his next move.

He was tired. He wanted to go home. But then he remembered the mess he had made. He decided he wasn't ready to face it and have to clean it up. Once the decision was made, he left. He got in his car and drove to the Best Western and rented a room for the night. The man knew he was tired with all that had happened today, but he didn't realize how tired. For once he got to his room and put his stuff on the table, he laid down on the bed thinking he would watch T.V. for a little while. But he immediately went to sleep and did not wake up once during the night.

Chloe sat up in her hospital bed. She was ready to leave, but the doctor wasn't quite ready to discharge her yet. He said she could walk around the floor if she wanted to. So she decided she would go see Detective Bonner. Chloe got out of bed, put her robe on and headed toward his room. The nurses looked up as she came out of her room.

"I know the doctor said you could go for a walk today, just don't overdo it." Sally said. "Would you like for me to go with you since this is your first time to venture out on your own?"

"I don't think so. I'm just going to Detective Bonner's room. How is he today?"

"About the same," was the answer from one of the nurses at the nurses' station.

The officer stationed at Detective Bonner's door knew Chloe so he let her in the room. He knew she had been shot at the same time and that they were both under protective custody. He also knew they were both lucky to be alive. He watched as Chloe went to the detective's bedside. She stood there several minutes then she turned around and pulled a chair close to the detective's bed and sat down.

After Chloe sat down, she took the detective's hand in hers and began to pray.

"Lord, there is so much going on I hardly know where to begin. But the thing is, I know that You do. Bob tried to save me and in doing so he is now fighting for his life. I ask You to be with him and fight for him. Amen."

The officer standing by the door listened as Chloe prayed for the detective. Julie had also come to see her husband, but not wanting to interrupt, she stood and waited until Chloe was finished. When Chloe said "Amen", Julie stepped into the room.

"Hi, Chloe. How are you doing today? I see you are up and about. That's good."

"I'm getting better all the time. I'm hoping they'll let me go home tomorrow, but I'm pretty sure that it's wishful thinking."

"Thank you for your prayer, Chloe. Julie said, when she reached her husband's side. She picked up his hand and repeated what Chloe had done, then she bent over and gave him a kiss on the cheek. Feeling Julie's lips on his cheek, Detective Bonner struggled to open his eyes.

"Bob? Bob?" Detective Bonner didn't answer, but he did look at her.

"Nurse. Sally! Hurry! My husband just opened his eyes."

Sally came into the room. She immediately checked all of the detective's vital signs. She watched him watch his wife's every move, then she immediately called the doctor.

Chloe backed out of the room while all the time, thanking God for working on the detective's behalf. On leaving the detective's room, she decided to return to her room. She was tired. A little more so than she thought she would have been.

"Mrs. Bonner, you don't really believe prayer works. Do you?" The officer guarding Detective Bonner's room asked.

"Of course I do. Why else would I pray? If you don't believe something is going to work, why would you ask for it?"

Just then the officer's replacement showed up.

"Would you like to talk about it, Officer Franklin?" Chloe asked, as she looked at his name tag.

"Yes. No. Maybe. Some other time."

"There's no time like the present. How about it?" Chloe turned around and began walking in the direction of the waiting room hoping that Officer Franklin would follow. He did. God's timing was always right on time.

CHAPTER 25

When the doctor entered Detective Bonner's room, Julie stepped to the side away from her husband. The doctor watched as the detective's eyes followed his wife's every movement.

"Detective Bonner, I am so glad to see you have decided to wake up today." The doctor said, as he watched the detective begin to watch his movements and then the nurses. It was a good sign. But he still hadn't spoken.

The detective's gaze went back to his wife. "Julie."

"Yes, Bob. I'm here." Julie answered, returning to her husband's side.

Detective Bonner was going to be just fine.

What prompted Chloe to go to the waiting room? She told herself she didn't know, but she did. In obedience (to God's prompting), she decided to go to the waiting room and see what happened. She was a little scared. She had never told anyone about Jesus before. She knew she believed, but what did she say to someone else to show them how important believing in Jesus was.

She sat down in the chair that was furthest from the door. If Officer Franklin was following her, she wanted him to have a quiet place where they could talk freely.

"Yes!" Chloe said to herself. For when she turned around to sit down, she found herself facing the officer. As he began to sit down, he pulled one of the chairs facing Chloe so they could have a private conversation.

"Oh, God. Please help me say the right words." Chloe said under her breath.

"Officer Franklin, do you know anything about Jesus? Anything at all?"

"Yes, Mrs. Kelley. I do. A little bit anyway. I wasn't raised in church. I went with friends every once in a while, but that was all. I try to believe, but I just don't."

"What part don't you believe?"

"I guess the part about Jesus dying for me. Why would He do that? And why are there supposed to be three in one? You know, the Father, the Son and the Holy Ghost."

"I'm a new Believer myself, but let's talk about the first question first. The answer is very simple. He loves you."

"I know people keep saying that. They say He took our sin and placed it on his back so we would not have to carry it. But, it makes no sense to me."

Chloe thought for a moment. This was going to be much harder than she thought.

"Officer Franklin, are you married?" Chloe asked softly.

"Yes, I am."

"Do you love your wife?"

"Of course, I do. What kind of question is that?"

"Why do you love your wife?" Chloe kept speaking softly while continually praying under her breath at the same time.

"I don't know. She makes my heart beat faster whenever I am around her."

"Go on."

"She feels as if she is a part of me. I want to be around her. She makes me happy. There are so many reasons."

"Okay. Do you have any kids?"

"Yes."

"Do you love them?"

"Yes, more than anything?"

"More than your wife?"

"Yes, and no. They are a part of us."

"So basically when you and your wife got married you became a part of each other. Then your kids became a part of you."

"Sounds good."

"You love them?"

"Yes."

"Why?"

"What kind of question is that?"

"Why do you love them?"

Officer Franklin took the question seriously and thought several minutes before he finally answered. "They are a part of me."

"If you accept Jesus, then He becomes a part of you. Everyday your relationship will grow deeper. Just as your relationship with your wife has grown since the day you married her. Your relationship with Jesus will keep growing in the same way."

"Would you give your life for your wife or your kids to save them?"

"Yes."

"That's exactly what Jesus did for you. He saved you from having to pay for your own sin when the debt came due. The important thing right now is for you to accept Jesus as your Savior. All the rest can come later over a period of time. Just as your relationship with your wife grew over a period of time. So your understanding of Jesus will do the same."

"Okay, maybe I should give it a try. What do I do?"

"It's really simple. You confess your sins, you ask Jesus to forgive you for those sins, you accept the fact that Jesus died on the cross to pay for your sins. Just say what is in your heart."

Chloe and Officer Franklin sat quietly for several minutes. Just as Chloe was about to give up, the officer spoke up.

"Jesus, I have heard all of these words spoken before. I want to believe. I really do. I am so sorry for all the sins I have committed. I ask Your forgiveness for each and every one. Thank you for dying for me and thank You for living for me, too. Amen."

"That was beautiful, Officer Franklin. Welcome into the Kingdom of God. You have just been given the most precious gift. The gift of eternal life. I am so happy for you."

"Thank you, Mrs. Kelley. But I best be getting home now. My wife is going to be wondering where I am and she is going to start to worry about me." Officer Franklin shook Chloe's hand holding it for a couple of seconds before letting it go. "Thanks," he said, as he walked away.

On the way home, Officer Franklin was so engrossed in reliving the moment of his salvation that he did not pick up on the fact that he was being followed. When he arrived at his house, he pulled directly into the garage, hitting the garage door button so the doors would come down behind him. He sat in the quiet of the car for several minutes enjoying what he had just been given. Eternal life.

He loved his wife and kids with all of his heart, but right at this moment in time he wanted to be alone. He wanted to keep on experiencing the love of God.

When several minutes had passed, and her husband had not come in the house, Linda, Officer Franklin's wife, opened the door between the house and the garage. Peering toward the window of the car she called out, "Honey, are you okay?"

"Yes, Linda. I'm fine. I am just fine."

"Okay, but supper is just about ready."

As Officer Franklin sat in the darkness of the garage thanking Jesus for His gift, he began to wonder how he was going to share this new found gift with Linda.

Finally he decided he'd better get out of the car and go into the house. When he entered, he gave his wife a big hug and a kiss. He then proceeded to go on into the living room. The kids were so engrossed in their cartoons they didn't even see him enter the room. After a minute, he backed quietly out of the room and returned to his wife. He stood there for several minutes watching her as she cooked. He walked over to the stove, turned the fire off under the burner and turned his wife around to face him.

"Franklin, what on earth is going on?"

"Linda, I was given a special gift today and I want to share it with you." Franklin said, as he stood facing his wife while looking straight into her eyes.

"Linda, what do you know about Jesus?"

The man pulled up across the street from Officer Franklin's house. He watched through the picture window as the officer stood talking to his wife. The picture window allowed him to see through the living room into the kitchen. It was always nice to have a plan "B". He didn't know how, but he might be able to use this officer to get to Chloe. Lady Luck placed him right in front of him while he was trying to figure out a plan. He had seen this officer talking to Chloe just before he'd gotten off his shift at the hospital. Now what they had been talking about in the corner of the waiting room, he didn't know. He just knew they seemed awfully close.

The man got out of his car and walked toward the house. Being very careful not to let anyone see him, he went through the gate into the backyard. It was a large backyard with toys scattered all over the place. He wasn't sure what it was, but he stumbled over one of the toys making a very loud noise when he caught himself to keep him from falling. Within seconds the backyard light came on and the officer came out on the back porch.

When the man saw the officer's gun, he immediately jumped over the gate. He then turned and immediately entered the neighbor's yard. Becoming very still, he stood and watched as the officer checked to see where the noise had come from. He finally located a wagon turned over on its side. He knew the kids could have left it that way, but somehow it just didn't feel right. He stood there then he bent over to stand the wagon upright. After a bit, he returned to the house.

The man returned to his car. He sat in silence mulling over how he could use this officer to gain access to Chloe, or even the

Detective for that matter. As he sat there staring at the house, the front porch light came on and the officer came outside and began looking all around. He had changed his clothes, but he still had the gun in his hand.

Office Franklin didn't know why, but he had the feeling he was being watched. His eyes began to search his front yard, then the street, then the neighbor's yards. He was checking to see if there was anything that should not be there. His eyes stopped on the man's car. He knew he had not seen this car before so he decided to check it out.

As he started toward the car, it sped off. As it left the scene, the man put his arm outside of the window and fired the gun held in his hand then watched as the officer fell to the ground.

Linda had called the police when her husband had gone outside and now she yelled into the phone. "Officer down! Oh, my God! Officer down!" Throwing the phone to the ground she ran to her husband.

CHAPTER 26

C hloe followed Seth to the elevator. After kissing him goodbye and giving him last minute instructions on what to bring the next day, she turned around to go back to her room. When she passed the nurses' station, she could hear the nurses whispering.

"What's going on?" Chloe asked.

"We don't really know." One of the nurses answered. "But we did hear that one of the officers that was up here guarding you or the detective was shot. He's in the emergency room right now. The thing is, we haven't heard who it is yet."

Chloe returned to her room and sat down on her bed thinking. She wished she knew who had been shot. It didn't really matter though because she didn't have to have someone's name to be able to pray for them. She hadn't heard anything more and she was getting really tired. Her last thought before she drifted off to sleep was for the officer who was laying in the emergency room.

After having surgery on his leg, Officer Franklin was put in the room on the other side of Detective Bonner's. A guard was also put on the outside of his room. Because two of the men that were shot were officers of the law and because Chloe had been shot at the same time as the detective, they had all been placed together under protective custody.

The detective that had been put on Detective Bonner's and Chloe's cases once they arrived in Lufkin was named Detective Wynan. He was a good Christian man and respected by those who knew him. He sat in the waiting room reading over the cases that had been faxed to him. While he sat reading the case files, he was alerted to the fact an officer that had been guarding one or both of his cases had also been shot and was in the emergency room. Gathering up his files, he handed the papers to the officer that was outside Mrs. Kelley's room and headed downstairs to the emergency room.

Detective Wynan stood talking to the nurse in the emergency room trying to find out the condition of the officer that had been shot. She could tell him nothing at this point. He turned to some of the officers that came when they heard the "Officer Down" call. They knew they couldn't stay long. Some had things that had to be done, but those who could, stayed.

Linda was also in the waiting room. She was waiting on word about her husband's condition. Her neighbor, Janet, came over to see if she could help. It was decided she would take the kids for the night. Linda needed to be with her husband.

She was tired. She was afraid. But what kept coming to her mind was what her husband had been telling her about Jesus. He hadn't had time to tell her much. Just enough to get her interested. It wasn't the amount of time he had, but it was what he said and the look on his face when he said it. But then her world came crashing down.

Chloe didn't know how long she had been asleep, but she woke up to a lot of commotion. Someone was being put in the room on the other side of Detective Bonner's room. The nurses were all busy getting the new occupant in the bed and comfortable. Chloe thought about the officer that had been shot so she decided to get up and go see what she could find out about his condition.

She waited until she thought no one would be paying attention to her and she headed toward his room.

"Where do you think you are going, Chloe?" Chloe's nurse called out just as the officer guarding her stepped forward.

"I was actually going to check on your new patient. Do you know who it is?"

"I believe his name is Officer Franklin."

"You know he was one of the officer's guarding us. Right?"

"Yes, Chloe, we know, but it's late and you need to go back to your room."

"I know. I know. I just felt like I was supposed to be out here."

"Well, go back to bed so we can finish settling Officer Franklin in his room."

"Okay. If I must."

"You must."

On hearing Chloe's name, Linda looked at her and asked, "Are you the one my husband was talking to this evening?"

Chloe looked at Linda and answered quietly, "If your husband is Officer Franklin, then, yes I am."

"Then please come sit with me for a minute. My husband was just beginning to tell me about Jesus and His precious gift when everything went wrong. He was so happy and now this. I don't know what to think, but could you please tell me what my husband was going to tell me."

"It was the gift of eternal life. By accepting the fact that Jesus died for our sins. We ask for His forgiveness for our sins. We accept the fact that Jesus died and rose from the dead. And He did it all for us. So that when we die, if we have accepted His gift, we will also rise from the dead to be with Him."

"My husband. He accepted this gift didn't he?"

"Yes, Linda, he did. He was so excited he could hardly wait to get home and tell you all about it."

"Chloe, what do I do to accept this gift of life?"

"Listen to your heart. Linda. When your heart and Jesus' heart become as one, you will have made your decision to follow Him. For it is with the heart one believeth unto salvation. Let me know when you're ready?"

"I'm ready."

"Jesus, I believe in You with all of my heart. What I don't know now, I ask You to teach me. Forgive me for my sins. Thank You for dying for me. And because I know You died and then rose from the dead, I know I will have eternal life with You in Heaven. Amen." Linda repeated each and every word after Chloe. And when she finished, she knew in her heart she meant every word.

"Lord, we also ask You to take care of Officer Franklin and keep him safe in Your care. Amen."

Linda mouthed a thank you to Chloe as she turned to follow one of the nurses to her husband's room. Chloe nodded then turned to go into her own room. Once again she was tired. She needed to get her rest for she felt sure she would be going home tomorrow. God was so good and He always had a plan.

Detective Wynan had been caught off guard. He had been sitting in the corner going over Chloe's file when Linda called out to her. He didn't know whether to say anything or not so he kept silent.

He smiled to himself as he listened to Linda accept Jesus as her Savior. He now knew what Detective Bonner saw in Chloe. As a detective, he couldn't just dismiss her, but she did go to the bottom of the list. The thing of it was he didn't even know what list. Her file was very confusing. With Detective Bonner regaining consciousness, he would be able to talk to him very soon.

He hoped to talk to Chloe one more time before she left the hospital. He knew the doctors were thinking about letting her go home tomorrow. Maybe she would remember something. Maybe something he said would jog her memory. At least he had to give it a try.

Once Chloe was released from the hospital, he was going to drive to Livingston and talk face to face with whoever was going to take over from him.

CHAPTER 27

Today was the day. Chloe was going home. Seth arrived at the hospital two hours early. He brought everything Chloe had on her list and then some. Just in case.

Chloe was all smiles when she watched Seth walk through her hospital door. She had already taken her bath. She was just waiting on her clean clothes and she would be ready to go home. She only had one problem. The doctor had not arrived. She didn't know for sure they were going to let her go home.

"Chloe, has the doctor been in yet?" Seth asked.

"Nope. And I think he is doing it on purpose. He knows how much I want to go home today."

"What am I doing on purpose, Chloe?" The doctor asked, entering Chloe's hospital room on cue. He walked over to Chloe's bed and began to take her vital signs. He checked her gunshot wound and was quite pleased with what he saw. He was going to let Chloe go home today, but first he was going to have a little fun.

"I don't know, Chloe. Your vitals are good, but your arm doesn't look as good as it did yesterday. Maybe we should put off you going home for one more day."

"What! You've got to be kidding!" Chloe said, and began searching the doctor's face for any sign that he might be kidding.

Dr. Crawford began showing her some of the red areas that caused him concern. He knew they were progressing just fine, but he was hoping she didn't.

During Chloe's stay at the hospital, she and Dr. Crawford had come to know each other pretty well, and were constantly pulling jokes on one another.

"Dr. Crawford, you are kidding me. Right?"

"Sorry, but no I'm not. One more day and you should be ready to go. By the way, what did I do on purpose?"

"You heard that, huh?"

"Yes, I did." Dr. Crawford said, with a smile on his face.

"Is this one of those gotcha moments? Do I really have to stay? Or do I get to go home?" Chloe asked, with a sad pucker on her face and tearful sound in her voice.

"Chloe, I'm sorry, but you really do have to stay one-------," but when Dr. Crawford saw Chloe's face, he decided the joke had gone far enough. So he looked at her and said.

"Gotcha!!!"

"So I really am going home. No kidding?"

"Yes, Chloe. You're really going home. No kidding."

As soon as Dr. Crawford said she was going home, the sad pucker Chloe had on her face turned into a smile and the tearful sound she had in her voice completely went away.

"Gotcha." Chloe said back at the doctor.

"Does she do this often?" Dr. Crawford asked, as he looked straight at Seth.

"When she wants to get her own way, yes."

"I'm going to miss you Chloe," the doctor said. "It's been a pleasure being one of your doctors, but I really do hope I don't see you in here again."

"Dr. Crawford, come to the ICU stat," the intercom said. It repeated those words three times in quick succession.

"Don't they know I'm already here?" He asked.

Dr. Crawford turned to Chloe and said, "It's been a pleasure, Chloe," then he turned and walked out the door.

"Bye, Dr. Crawford."

And he was gone.

"Well, Chloe, are you going home with me today or what?" Seth asked.

"I am! I am! I am! Why don't you go finish the paperwork while I get out of this hospital gown." Chloe said, enthusiastically.

"I sure am glad you're coming home." Seth answered, smiling at his wife as he left the room and headed toward the nurses' station.

"Me, too!" Chloe exclaimed. So happy she could hardly contain her excitement.

When Chloe finished dressing, and Seth finished with the paperwork, they decided to go see Detective Bonner before they left. But when they headed that direction, one of the nurses called out, "Chloe, I think the detective is asleep right now."

"How is he doing?"

"He's doing really good. Once he came out of his coma, he was on the road to recovery."

Seth went to Detective Bonner's room just to check on him and came back shaking his head yes.

Chloe asked one of the nurses for a piece of paper and left Detective Bonner a note to read once he woke up.

The man watched as Chloe and Seth exited the hospital. He found a parking space close enough to the exit door so he could sit in his car and wait. He found out they were going to release Chloe sometime today. So he had bought a book, pushed his seat back and settled in to wait.

"Chloe, do you want to stop somewhere and eat?"

"I don't think so, Seth. I just want to go home."

"Aren't you just the least bit hungry?"

"Yes, I am, but I want to go home."

"Okay. Why don't I drive through Chick-Fil-A and you can eat on the way home?"

"Now, that sounds like a good idea."

The man followed the Kelley's until Seth pulled into Chick-Fil-A, but he decided to keep on going. He knew where they were going. He would just beat them to the house and get settled in before they got there.

While he sat there waiting for Chloe to get home, he was thinking to himself that this had gone on way too long. He had to come up with a plan to end it once and for all.

It had been so long he wasn't even sure what the plan had been in the beginning. He hadn't been there. But now he was. He did know one thing. Every time he decided to act, something came between him and Chloe. Maybe he should just give up and find someone else. There was always Chloe's friend Julie. The only problem was her husband was a detective.

"What to do? What to do?"

While the man sat there trying to decide on his plan of action, Chloe and Seth arrived.

"Boy! It's great to be home." Chloe said, as Seth helped her out of the car and into the house.

"I had all sorts of plans on what I would do when I got home, but I think I am really tired."

"Why don't you sit in your recliner and take a nap while I get the stuff out of the car?"

"Okay. I think I will." Chloe said, as she sat down and pushed her chair back to its reclining position. Seth picked up Chloe's favorite blanket and covered her up. Then went to get the stuff out of the car.

"What to do? What to do?" The man couldn't think of a plan, but he didn't want to give up either. So he sat in his favorite hiding place filled with indecision. He was tired and he didn't think Chloe would come outside today. So he decided to go home. Giving the house one last look, he headed toward his motorcycle. He heard the neighbor's dogs barking in the distance and not knowing whether they were tied up or not he quickened his steps.

Next morning bright and early the man was back in place. He now had a plan and it was perfect. During the night he had decided he was not a quitter. Julie could wait until later. He would finish with Chloe first.

He didn't know if Chloe would come out today or not, but since she had been cooped up in the hospital for awhile, his guess was that as soon as it was light outside, she would be out on the back patio.

It was a beautiful day and the man didn't have to wait long. It wasn't as early as usual, but she had been in the hospital. Still, she was here and that was all that counted.

"Seth, come on outside." Chloe called her husband from the patio.

Chloe washed off the patio table, got the cushion for her chair and went back to get her Bible. She sat down and as she did, she was filled with such a feeling of thankfulness that all she could do was to thank God for saving her. And not only her, but Seth and Detective Bonner, plus Officer Franklin.

Seth came to the patio door and asked her if she would like a cup of hot chocolate.

"That would be great, Seth." Chloe said, as she placed her Bible on the table then laid her head back and enjoyed the sun. After a couple of minutes, Seth reappeared with two cups of hot chocolate in his hands.

"Here's your hot chocolate, my lady." Seth bowed, put her chocolate on the table in front of her, and gave her a big kiss.

"Chloe, would you like to go for a short walk? It's a beautiful day and it's probably good for you."

"I don't know, Seth. Let me think about it."

Seth left Chloe alone for about thirty minutes and then he returned.

"Okay, Chloe. Are you ready to go?"

"Yes, I think I will. I have already been walking in the hospital so this should be a piece of cake. Right?"

Seth went in the house to get Chloe's jacket. When he returned, he helped her put it on. As she zipped it up, she grabbed Seth's hand and headed for the woods. She knew she had to sooner or later and it might as well be now.

The man smiled. Lady Luck was smiling on him today. Last night he had figured out a plan and it was a really good plan. But when Lady Luck stepped in, even the best of plans were subject to change.

He watched as Seth and Chloe started their walk. They were following the same path Seth had cut out for Chloe before she had gone into the hospital. Since they had been gone for a while, everything had grown higher and thicker.

"Chloe, why don't we wait until I get a chance to mow before we walk this way."

"I think it's okay for now, but I think you're right. You probably need to mow it before we walk this way again."

They were headed in his direction. He went very still and just waited.

CHAPTER 28

"It's something about the trees," Detective Bonner said out loud. He had been sitting in the chair, next to his bed, in his hospital room when he stood up, closed his eyes and tried to recall something he knew was important. He was also sure it had something to do with Chloe's case. But the memory stayed just out of his reach.

"Why don't they answer?" Detective Bonner asked out loud, but to no one in particular. He needed to talk to Seth first, because Seth was the one with Chloe. He called both Seth and Chloe's cell phones. Then he called the house phone. Still no answer.

Seth and Chloe heard the phone in the distance. But knowing they couldn't reach it in time, they decided to let the answering machine get it.

"Chloe, did you bring your cell phone?"

"I didn't even think of it. How about you?"

"Me either."

"Maybe we should go back?" Just as Chloe finished speaking, the man dropped out of the tree knocking Seth to the ground.

He picked up a large branch and knocked Seth unconscious with it.

"Hello, Chloe," the man said, as he smiled at her. "You've been having some pretty rough days. Haven't you?"

"I guess you could say that."

The man retrieved his gun from the holster on his ankle and pointed it at Chloe.

"Now you're going to go with me, but we are going to have to take your car."

"Where are you going to take me?" Chloe asked, her voice trembling so much he could hardly understand her.

"That's for me to know and for you to find out. Very soon." The man laughed as he pushed Chloe toward the house.

"Why doesn't anyone answer their phones?" Detective Bonner asked out loud. Using a few colorful words. First, because he had remembered something very important to the case. And second, because he couldn't reach anyone on his phone to relay this new information to. As soon as the words left his mouth, he was sorry.

"I am so sorry, Lord. Please forgive me." Detective Bonner said contritely.

The nurses at the nurses' station heard Detective Bonner. They looked at each other with questioning looks on their faces. Not once from the moment he had been brought in up until now, had he even come close to saying something even a little off color.

"What is wrong, Detective? How can we help?"

"I'm sorry ladies, I really am, but I can't seem to find anyone and I am afraid Chloe is in danger once again."

"I saw Detective Wynan in the waiting room." Sally said.

"Do you want me to see if he's still there?"

"Yes, Sally. Please. And hurry."

Sally left to see if she could find Detective Wynan. She went to the waiting room hoping he was still there. He was. Sally walked toward the detective just as he was shaking some man's hand telling him thank you and goodbye.

"Hi, Sally. How are you today?" Detective Wynan asked the young girl.

"Detective Bonner is trying to get a hold of you. He thinks Chloe is in danger and no one is answering their house or cell phones."

"Thanks, Sally." The detective said, heading toward Detective Bonner's room while at the same time retrieving his phone from his pocket. He'd just gotten himself a new phone with all the bells and whistles and after looking at it, he found he had accidentally turned it off instead of on silent.

"Sorry, Bob. What's up? Sally said you were trying to get hold of me."

Detective Bonner told Detective Wynan what he had remembered.

"I tried to get hold of Detective Roberts. I wanted him to check out the woods behind Chloe's house. It's the trees. He has been up in the trees. He's not in the bushes on the ground. He has been up in the trees. At least, some of the time. All of the times we have been called to check out the woods behind Chloe's house, not once did we look up in the trees. We did find traces of someone on the ground, though."

Detective Bonner could see the confused look on Detective Wynan's face so he decided to start from the beginning, but first he had to try Seth and Chloe again. He needed to warn them. Then he needed to call Detective Roberts and have him drive out to the Kelley's house and check on them. He was having one of his gut feelings again and he didn't like it.

"Sorry, Detective Wynan. I need to make one more phone call."

"Hello." Detective Roberts answered.

"It's the trees. Up in the trees. Not on the ground. I tried to reach Seth and Chloe, but no one is answering."

"Hello, to you, too, Bob, and I'll get right on it. I'll call you back later."

"Thanks, I appreciate it." Hanging up he looked at Detective Wynan.

"I'm sorry, Cameron. I know you are limited as to what you can do, but I couldn't get hold of anyone else."

"I've only heard part of what's going on. Why don't you fill me in. At least the part I might be able to help you with."

Detective Bonner started at the beginning filling Detective Wynan in with everything he knew.

"Wow! Chloe and her husband have been having a really hard time the last couple of years. And during that time your families became friends, too." Detective Wynan said, after Detective Bonner finished his story.

"Yes, and that is why I am so worried about Seth and Chloe."

"If I can help you in any way? Please, just let me know. Right now, I'm just not sure how I can."

"Thanks, I appreciate it." Just then Detective Bonner's cell phone rang. Answering it, he waved at Detective Wynan as he walked out the door.

"Bob, I am almost to the Kelley's house. I think I passed the Kelley's car, but I am not sure. We were turning off on to the dirt road that leads to their house and they were turning on to the highway. The driver looked like Mrs. Kelley, but the person on the passenger side did not look like Mr. Kelley."

"Man, I wish I was there. How many cars do you have with you?"

"Three including myself."

"I think you need to turn around and follow Mrs. Kelley. Take one car with you and send one car to the Kelley's house. Mr. Kelley may be in trouble."

Detective Robert's turned around to follow the car Chloe was in while talking to Detective Bonner. He stopped, made the motion for one to follow him and the other to continue on.

After giving Detective Roberts the information, Detective Bonner disconnected his cell phone. He knew Detective Roberts would call him as soon as possible. Sitting here waiting while everyone else did all the work was the pits.

———————

The man pushed his gun deep into Chloe's side as they watched Detective Roberts make the turn from the highway onto the dirt road. Chloe slowed but did not stop as she pulled from the dirt road onto the highway.

When the detective saw Chloe, he immediately looked over at the passenger's side expecting to see Mr. Kelley. Not seeing who he thought he was going to see in the passenger's seat made him question if he had really seen Mrs. Kelley.

Since there were two cars behind Detective Roberts, he did not have time for a second look before the car Mrs. Kelley was in was gone.

The man saw the split second look between Chloe and Detective Roberts. Recognition. Then on Chloe's face, hope.

"Speed up, Chloe. We need to get farther down the road in case the detective decides he needs to turn around and follow us." The man said, pressing the gun deeper into Chloe's side.

"Faster, Chloe. I am not concerned about the speed limit. We're not going to stop anyway." The man said, as he pushed the gun into Chloe's side once again. Only this time he pressed a little harder than he had before. He knew that one of the cars that made the turn in front of them would, in a few minutes at the most, try to turn around, catch up with them, and follow them.

The man was glad when a change of plans presented itself. Which plan was the best he didn't know. What he did know was that this plan was already in motion when he arrived. He sat there watching as the new plan evolved. He was not one to pass up a good opportunity.

"Speed up, Chloe."

"I can't go any faster. If I do, there is no telling what will happen."

He could see the truth in the words she spoke for it was at that very moment the car began to wobble.

"Okay, you can slow down. A little bit. Only a little bit." He watched as Chloe regained control of the car. He now had a decision to make. He knew he either needed Chloe to pull over and let him drive, or have Chloe pull over and stop on one of the many side roads along the highway.

The man turned around and looked intently at the road behind them. Seeing no one on the road, he knew this was probably the best opportunity he was going to have.

"Slow down, Chloe. There." The man said. "Pull over, turn around and park in that little stand of trees. That should serve my purpose very well."

As Chloe did what she was told, she began to lose all hope of being found. She thought the detective had seen her, but she knew they couldn't be seen by a passing car from the highway. The bushes and the little stand of trees covered them completely.

"Oh, Lord." Chloe said to herself. "I am in so much trouble."

When Chloe finished her little prayer the man laughed and spoke out loud.

"There he goes. Too bad, Chloe. I guess he didn't see you after all."

CHAPTER 29

When the police arrived at the Kelley's house, the garage doors were open and one of the cars was missing. Both officers, Officer Moore and Officer Reyes, got out of their cars and started looking around. Officer Moore went to the front of the house, checked the front door to see if it was unlocked, and found it wasn't and then started toward the back. Before they separated they decided they would meet on the other side of the house by the swimming pool. Officer Reyes was to check the area by the barn and then proceed to the swimming pool.

As each officer covered their assigned territory and met by the pool, they looked at each other shaking their heads. They retreated to the patio where they stood talking. Officer Reyes went to the patio door and knocked. Since there was no answer, he pulled at the door just to make sure it was locked and found that it wasn't.

"I don't think the Kelley's would have left this door open and then left."

"Maybe, they just forgot." The other officer said.

"With all that has been going on in Mrs. Kelley's life, I don't think so."

Both officers headed toward the woods. This time with their guns drawn. They weren't going to be caught off guard. They approached the woods quietly, searching every bush or small tree that could hide someone behind it. They could tell Seth had at one time mowed a path for Chloe, but now it had grown over. As they continued forward, one of the officers almost stepped on Seth.

They checked for injuries to see if an ambulance was needed. Officer Reyes asked Officer Moore to run to the house and bring back a wet cloth.

"Hurry Jack, if we can't bring him to, we'll have to take him to the hospital."

After a couple of minutes, Seth opened his eyes and on seeing Officer Reyes he said, "Hi, Officer Reyes, Fancy meeting you here." Seth tried to grin, but found that movement made his head hurt more than it already did. He raised his hand to his head and as he did, he touched a very large knot. Not much blood, but a very large knot.

Officer Moore returned with the wet cloth and handed it to Seth.

"Seth, this is Officer Moore. I had him run up to the house to get you a wet rag." Officer Reyes stuck his hand out to pull Seth to a standing position.

"I'm fine." Seth said, winching as he stood up.

"Do you think you can make it back to the house, or do we need to call an ambulance?"

"I'm fine, Officer Reyes. I just have a whopper of a headache." Seth held his head, walking toward the house with slow but determined steps.

After finding out that Chloe was still missing, Seth began telling his story to the officers. They reached the patio and Seth decided he needed to sit down and catch his breath.

"What do we do now? Where do we start? How do we find Chloe?" Seth said, after he finished his story.

"If you feel alright, we need to go to the station and see if we can get some answers there. You don't need to be driving nor do you need to be by yourself."

"Fine. I don't know what I'm supposed to be doing anyway."

As Seth got into the back seat, his mind would not settle down on any one thing. In his confusion, Seth's mind settled on one Bible verse II Timothy 1:7. *"For God hath not given us the spirit of fear, but of power, and of love, and of a sound mind."*

Seth started praying first and foremost for Chloe. As he prayed, he wondered how those people who did not know God made it through a normal day much less a day filled with torment.

CHAPTER 30

"Are we going to stay here all day?" Chloe asked the man, as they sat in silence watching all the cars go by.

The man didn't say anything. He just sat there. His silence made Chloe very nervous and uncomfortable. She did not look at him and he did not look at her. They both stared straight ahead. First they saw Detective Roberts go by. She wanted to call out to him, but she knew he wouldn't hear her.

Chloe thought it was strange that after the police cars passed, they continued to sit there. An hour or so later they were still sitting there. What was going on?

Chloe was tired of sitting in one position. Her legs were going to sleep, but she didn't know if she dared move or not. Not wanting to take the chance of making him mad she didn't say anything. She didn't know how much time had passed, but after a very long time, Chloe saw another police car go by. There were two officers in the front, but there was also someone sitting in the back seat. She wondered if it was Seth. She hoped it was. Because if it was, that meant he was still alive.

"I can't believe it. Once again your husband comes out on top. I am no longer going to use up my energy on him. I am now going to pretend he just does not exist. It is just you and me from now on." The man turned and smiled in Chloe's direction.

Chloe stared straight ahead. She didn't want to look at him. She didn't want to see his gloating, smiling face. All she wanted to do was cry, but she wasn't going to give him the satisfaction.

"Well, Chloe, I guess it's time to head for home. I think everyone who could have helped you is long gone. Don't you think? I have covered my tracks pretty good. There is no help coming your way. You're mine now. All mine."

"God, where are You? I sure am in a whole lot of trouble here." Chloe thought to herself. Once again her thoughts were interrupted.

"It's time to leave, Chloe. You need to drive toward town. You must go the speed limit. We don't need to get pulled over for going too fast. Now do we? Once we get there, I'll give you directions."

Chloe pulled out on the highway thankful for the silence that ensued. She wanted to be able to talk to God. She needed to talk to Him.

"Praying are you, Chloe?" The man asked, as he interrupted her thoughts once again. She really wished he would shut up. "Do you really think God can help you now? No one knows where you are. No one knows where we are going. So how is this God that you keep praying to, going to help you now?"

"I don't know, but He will."

"Shut up." The man said, as he put the gun to Chloe's head.

Chloe stopped talking. She didn't want to antagonize him anymore than she already had. She may have stopped talking out loud, but inside she was calling out to her God. She knew in her heart that her God was capable of getting her out of any trouble she might be in. He had done it before and He could do it again.

As the car approached town, peace settled over Chloe. She instantly knew what it was. It was the peace that could only come from God. She was calm while she followed the man's directions.

He smiled at Chloe as he told her to pull in the driveway. She pulled in slowly coming to a stop just short of the garage doors. She looked around realizing she had been here before. They both got out of the car. The man told her to stop and wait for him. She wanted to run, but she knew she couldn't outrun a bullet.

The man got to her side, took her by the arm and led her toward the front door. Chloe kept looking around. She knew she had been here before. All of a sudden she remembered.

"Oh, no! It can't be."

"Yes, Chloe. Yes, it can."

"I can't believe we lost him?" Someone yelled out in their frustration.

"I can't either, but he's gone so now let's focus. We need to start from the beginning. The faster we get at it, the faster we bring Mrs. Kelley home."

Detective Bonner and Julie were standing at the door smiling. Everyone in the room was so focused on trying to find a clue that would help with the case, they had not seen the detective and Julie enter the room. They stood there wondering how long it would take before someone realized they were in the room.

"Hey, Bob! What are you doing here?" Seth said, as he happened to look up. When everyone heard Seth, all eyes turned toward the door. Then everyone rushed forward welcoming them back. Seth waited until the last.

"Bob, I am so glad you are back. Somehow, somewhere we got off the track and Chloe's out there with a lunatic and we don't know how to find her."

"Come on, Seth. Let's sit down and think this thing through. I haven't done anything for the last few days but think about Chloe's case."

Julie was still standing at the door. She was so happy her husband was out of the hospital. She hoped she had not made a mistake by bringing him to the station. She knew her husband and she knew he would just sit and wonder what was going on. He needed to be in the thick of things. She knew it sounded crazy, but her husband would probably get more rest here than at home wanting to be here so she slipped quietly out the door leaving her husband in the care of a handful of men.

It didn't take long for the room to settle down and everyone to get back to business.

"I am really glad you're back." Detective Roberts said shaking his partner's hand. "To tell you the truth I'm at a dead end. Everybody is working hard. We just don't have any leads."

"Thanks, Kyle, it's great to be back. And if you're sure you don't mind, I would be happy to take this case back."

"I don't mind at all. It is now officially yours. Thanks."

Before the Bonner's had entered the room everyone had been busy. Now as things got back to normal, they each began to attack the papers in front of them. Looking for that one clue that could help break the case.

"Are you sure you're up to this, Bob? You know you just got out of the hospital."

"Oh, no!" The detective said, as he looked toward the door. No, Julie. He didn't even know how long she had been gone. He groaned because he realized it had to have been more than just a little while.

"Give me a second, Seth. I've got to call Julie." Detective Bonner motioned to Seth since they had just sat down to go over the file once again.

Detective Bonner picked up his cell phone and pressed Julie's number.

"I wondered how long it would take you to realize I was gone." Julie said, as she answered her cell phone.

"I am so sorry, Julie. I don't know what happened. I guess I just got carried away in the moment."

"It's okay, Bob." Julie laughed. "I know you love me and I know how much you want to help Chloe. I want you to help her, too. I ran a couple of errands and now I'm headed to pick up the kids. By the time I pick them up you should be ready to come home."

"Everyone is going to work overtime tonight, Julie. Chloe's life is hanging in the balance. I'll either call you to come get me or hitch a ride with someone else. That's probably the better option, because once you pick up the kids and get settled in at home, you're not going to want to get out again. Especially with the kids. How about we leave it at that. I'll just have someone drive me home."

"That's fine, Bob. Just remember. You just got out of the hospital and you can't help Chloe if you end up back in the hospital." Julie said making her husband promise not to stay too late.

Julie pulled over at the Conoco Station, which just happened to be the one that faced the street that went straight through town, while she talked to her husband. She was a fanatic about talking while driving. After she hung up, she decided to check her grocery list one more time to make sure she hadn't forgotten anything. While sitting there, Julie just happened to look up as Chloe's car drove by. She pulled out behind it as fast as she could. She wanted to follow it a safe distance behind without letting anyone know they were being followed. Not even Chloe.

Detective Bonner's phone rang. He was startled to hear Julie on the other end. "Bob, no talking just listen. I am following Chloe's car." The detective listened carefully while Julie explained what she had just seen. The moment she finished talking he got everyone moving.

"Seth and Detective Bonner both had to ride with Detective Roberts. Neither one had their own car. As Julie, relayed the direction she was going, Detective Bonner immediately told Detective Roberts what direction to take.

Everyone was filled with hope. At least at this point they knew she was still alive. She was in the hands of her kidnapper, but she was still alive.

Seth sat in the backseat praying. At the same time, he was in complete awe. God had just given them a miracle. He had given them hope when there was no hope. What a mighty God they served. The night was not over, but at least they had a chance for their tomorrows.

"Detective Roberts, would you get a move on it?" Detective Bonner said, while relaying Julie's directions.

"He's slowing down, Bob. What do I do? He's pulled in a driveway, but I can't see the address."

"Julie, just drive on by. I don't want you getting hurt."

"But what if he's just turning around or something? What if I lose him?"

"Julie, it's okay. We're right behind you. Step on your brake lights so I can be sure your car is the one in front of us."

Julie stepped on her brakes letting her husband know it was her while at the same time it was letting them know they should be looking for Chloe's car. They were so intent on following Julie's instructions; they didn't realize they had been there before.

"Bob, do you realize whose house this is?" Seth asked, as they quietly pulled into the driveway.

"Chloe brought me here several weeks after the last incident."

Detective Bonner spoke into the radio alerting everyone to the significance of whose house this was.

"I don't know if that's important, but it is information."

Seth looked at both Detective's. "What's the plan?"

Chloe's eyes had been continually looking for a way to escape. She was sure no one knew where she was and the street had been silent and still ever since they had pulled up into the driveway. Tears came to her eyes. Not knowing God's plan for you, always made it extra hard to hold on.

As much trouble as she knew she was in, Chloe still felt at peace. And when the fear threatened to overcome her, she was still able to remain calm.

"Move." The man said, as he pushed Chloe toward the door. She stumbled and when she righted herself, Chloe glanced in the direction of the street. That was when she thought she saw Julie's car. For a moment her hopes soared, then they plummeted just as quick, for the car kept going without even slowing down. She guessed she was wrong. It hadn't been Julie's car after all.

"You know. All your praying is going to get you nowhere. You know that, right?"

"No, I don't know that. I know my God is in control of this situation no matter what you may think." Chloe said, as they entered the house going to the kitchen. He pulled a chair away from the table and told her to sit down.

"You think your God is in control, but I'm the one holding the gun. I'm the one who has you here, and no one knows where you are."

"Yes, He does. You just don't know it yet. I know this is the house that belonged to Seth Delaney. Why are we here? And who are you?"

The man grabbed another chair and sat down in front of her. At the same time, he pulled off the fake beard, the fake sideburns and the bushy eyebrows. When he finished removing it all, she simply stared at him.

"It can't be." Chloe said. "You're dead."

"Haven't figured it out, have you?" He said, laughing hysterically. "The look on your face is worth all the trouble you put me through."

Chloe opened her mouth in complete disbelief. She sat in front of an exact replica of Sean Delay. She knew Delaney was dead so this man standing in front of her had to be a twin. An identical twin.

"You're a twin," Chloe couldn't help but stare at the man standing in front of her. "That explains so many things."

"Yes, Chloe. I am a twin. It has been fun, but now I am tiring of the game."

"At least tell me your name."

"Clay. Clay Delaney."

Clay had sat back in his chair making it unstable. Chloe saw her chance. She raised both of her feet and pushed at Clay's chair just as hard as she could. It tipped over and sent him sprawling on the floor. As soon as Clay lost his balance, Chloe was off and running. She headed for the front door. Thankfully, Clay had not locked the front door behind him. She pulled it open and ran as fast as she could for her freedom.

She heard Clay he hit the floor. He was right behind her. She could feel him breathing down her neck but couldn't tell how close he was.

"You are not going to get away, Chloe," were the last words Chloe heard as she ran out the door.

CHAPTER 31

Detective Bonner, Detective Roberts and all the other officers had exited their cars quietly. Knowing there was no way Seth was going to stay quiet in the car, Detective Bonner told him to stay close to him.

They all pulled their guns. They separated and headed toward the front and back doors when they heard the commotion inside. The door opened and out ran Chloe at full speed. She got to the center of the yard and tripped on something which sent her sprawling in the grass.

"I told you. You couldn't get away from me." The man said, as he raised his gun. "Your God cannot save you now."

It was dark and Clay could not see the officers and the detectives that stood just beyond where Chloe had fallen. Chloe falling gave Detective Bonner a clear shot at Clay.

"Stay down, Chloe." Detective Bonner said, just before he shot Clay three times in the chest.

As she lay on the ground, Chloe heard someone yell stay down. She had also heard the three shots, but Chloe was afraid to move.

"It's okay, Chloe." Seth told his wife soothingly.

"Detective Bonner shot the man who kidnapped you. You're safe." Seth reached down and pulled Chloe to her feet. He pulled her into his arms and stood there holding her close.

They both walked over to where Clay Delaney lay. He wasn't dead yet and there was an ambulance on the way, but no one thought he would live long enough for the ambulance to arrive.

Clay looked at Chloe and said, "I guess you win, for now."

"I guess I do."

"What did he mean by that?" Seth looked at Chloe with a quizzical expression his face.

"I'll tell you later. Can we just go home."

———

Seth and Chloe arrived at the police station bright and early the next morning. They had not stayed until the ambulance came. They didn't know if Clay Delaney was dead or not. It was going to be a long day, but they would face each problem as it arose.

"Good Morning, everyone!" Seth and Chloe both said, after entering the squad room. They saw Detective Bonner sitting at his desk and headed in his direction.

"Bye, honey." Detective Bonner told his wife as he watched the Kelley's approach.

"How are you two doing?" He asked.

"Pretty good. I guess." Chloe said, a little hesitantly.

"It doesn't sound as if you two had a very good night."

"Nope. Not at all. We actually haven't even discussed the events of last night. And this morning, she avoids all conversation headed in that direction."

"Seth, that's probably pretty normal. She's been through a lot." Detective Bonner commented softly.

"Chloe, you know we are going to have to go over all the things that happened to you from beginning to end. He's dead, Chloe. He can't hurt you anymore. But to close this case we need you to give us a statement."

Just then Julie walked through the door. She had been really worried about her friend and was glad when her husband called and said Chloe was at the station.

When Chloe saw Julie, she went to her friend. Julie held her giving her the support she needed at that moment.

After giving Chloe a hug, they both walked toward her husband's desk. Seth and Detective Bonner got some extra chairs so they could all sit together. After everyone was comfortable, Detective Bonner looked Chloe straight in the eyes and asked, "Are you ready for this, Chloe?"

"I'm as ready as I'll ever be." Chloe answered and began her story. Step by step from the time Clay jumped out of the tree knocking Seth unconscious to seeing Julie in the parking lot.

Chloe had to start over several times while writing her statement so Detective Bonner finally asked someone to come over and take dictation.

"I can't seem to remember anything after seeing Julie and praying real hard that she would see me." Chloe said, nearing the end of her statement. "I do remember Clay laughing at me all the time because I kept praying. Then as we passed the gas station, I saw Julie, but I couldn't tell if she saw me. He didn't see her though." Chloe looked at Julie and continued talking. "Did you see me, Julie? Were you the answer to my prayer?"

"I don't think I get that distinction, Chloe. But I did see you and I called Bob. I took off and followed you all the way to that house, giving Bob directions so he could find you. You pulled in the driveway and he went over and pulled you out. I drove on by, but I stepped on my brakes so Bob would know for sure that I was the one in front of him. I kept going, but by then they knew where you were. I was afraid the man had seen me and I was so afraid for you."

"I thought I saw you, Julie. But because of where we were, I thought maybe it wasn't your car. I thought it was just wishful thinking. But seeing what I thought was your car gave me hope. I felt as if I wasn't all alone." Chloe said sadly.

"Julie, I am so sorry. After all you've done for me, I didn't even thank you. You were the answer to my prayer."

"Okay, Chloe." Detective Bonner said interrupting the two friends. "Let's get back to after you saw Julie."

Once again Chloe started going over and over in her mind what had happened to her from the point when she had caught her first glimpse of Julie.

"Bob. You did say Clay Delaney was dead. Right?"

"Yes, Chloe. Clay Delaney is dead. I promise you that."

It was going to take someone a little while to type Chloe's statement so the four of them decided to go for a sandwich. They sat and talked as old friends do, but they completely avoided the subject of yesterday. They had been there an hour and decided it was time to go back and finish the task at hand.

All four had arrived back at the station. The statement had been completed. Chloe read over it and signed it. They were saying their goodbyes just inside the door when Chloe stopped.

"One question before we go, Bob."

"Sure. I hope it's one I can answer."

"When I looked at Clay Delaney, after he had been shot, he looked at me and said 'You win'. He waited a few seconds and then said 'For now'. What did he mean by that?"

"I don't know, Chloe. I wish I did. I don't even know what 'You win' meant."

"That one's easy. He kept telling me God wasn't going to help me and I kept telling him that yes He was. And He did."

Standing there with Chloe's question hanging in the air, the hairs on the back of his neck stood up once again. It startled him. He was among fellow officers, detectives, and friends. He was in the middle of a police station. All of these men had helped him save Chloe from her kidnapper. He didn't want to, but he turned to Chloe to get her reaction.

She looked him straight in the eyes, but said nothing. She had turned pale, but she turned to Seth and said, "Let's go. See you later, Julie. Thanks, I owe you my life."

Julie left at the same time Seth and Chloe did. Detective Bonner still needed to finish his report.

Detective Bonner tipped his chair back against the wall. The two front legs were up in the air with his legs wrapped around them. He locked his hands behind his head and closed his eyes. Everyone in the room knew this position well. It meant leave me alone I am thinking and I do not want to be bothered.

Chloe's case was still bothering him. He couldn't get all the facts pieced together. They just didn't fit. John Bledsoe, Sean Delaney and Clay Delaney had all been killed. The fact Sean and Clay had been twins filled in the answer to a lot of questions that were roaming around in his head.

His final report needed to be written so the case could be officially closed. But something kept bothering him. He kept remembering Clay as he lay there dying. When Chloe walked up to him, he looked her in the face and said, "You win... For now." The for now had been much softer, almost under his breath.

The one thought that was bothering him at the moment was when they had returned from the S&S Café just a little while ago. Chloe had sat down to read over and then sign her official statement. As he watched, the hairs on the back of his neck stood up. He couldn't believe it. Not here, not now. He was among fellow officers and friends. Chloe called it her intuition. He called it his gut feeling. Whatever it was, it shouldn't be happening now. He looked at Chloe, she had raised her head and was looking at him. She had turned pale and from the expression on her face, she knew she had felt it, too.

Detective Bonner wasn't ready to close the case, but the higher-ups wanted it over so he could move on to something else. So, he would officially do what he was told. Unofficially, he would make copies of Chloe's file. The unofficial one he would keep on his desk or at home in his personal file.

Seeming to have made a decision Detective Bonner opened his eyes, plopped the two front legs of his chair back down on the floor making a loud scraping noise and pulled out his notebook and started writing furiously on its white pages.

Everyone looked over in his direction, but then they returned to what they had been doing deciding now was not the time to ask questions.

Detective Bonner decided to stay late. He told everyone he just had to put some finishing touches on his report, but in truth, he needed to get the copies made for his own personal file. He said goodbye to each one as they left. The last one to leave was Detective Roberts.

"Bob, do you need help finishing up?"

"No, I've got it. You go on home. I told Julie we would go out to eat so I can't be late. You know how wives are."

"No, I don't. But I'll leave you to yourself."

Detective Bonner finished his official report within fifteen minutes. Then he took the file to the copy machine. Whether it seemed to be important or not, he made a copy of everything. What he couldn't get in the copier to document, he had taken pictures of earlier with his trusty but old fashioned Polaroid Camera. He wanted his file to contain any and all information gathered on Chloe's case in one place. Later, he would add his different thoughts on different things contained within the file.

"Julie, are you and the kids ready to meet me somewhere for dinner?" Detective Bonner asked, after having placed his call. "And, where would you like to go?"

"Why don't you just come home and we'll order out. How does that sound?"

"It sounds fine to me. Are you feeling okay?"

"Not really. How about we talk when you get home?"

Detective Bonner picked up his file and headed for the door. He decided he would stop for pizza. That way the kids would be fed, but Julie could talk to him about whatever was bothering her.

He stopped at Little Caesars on his way home and picked up two pizzas. Then he headed for home.

As he pulled into the driveway, Julie walked out the front door and met him on the steps. He grabbed the pizza's and they walked into the house.

"Hey, kids! Pizza."

"Yea!" Both kids yelled while running toward their dad at the same time.

"How about we go to the table first?" Their dad asked, placing the pizza on the kitchen table. As he did so, four hands reached toward the pizza.

"What are you two forgetting?"

"We need to pray first," Bobby Jr. answered his dad.

"You're right. Would you like to say the prayer?" The detective asked, as he looked toward Bobby Jr.

"Thank you for our pizza. Amen."

"I guess you two are hungry, huh?"

"Yes, Daddy." His daughter, Tiffany replied.

"Well, I need to talk to your mom for a minute. So you two go ahead and eat. Okay?"

"Sure, Daddy." They both said at the same time.

Julie had gotten both kids some milk and placed it on the table in front of them. She started to get them a piece of pizza, but noticed each one already had two pieces on their plate.

Detective Bonner and his wife turned to leave the room, when Tiffany said to her dad, "Mommy is sad today."

"Thanks, Tiffany. That's why your mommy and I are going to talk. So you and your brother go ahead and eat. Is that okay?"

"Sure, Daddy. I'm hungry."

Detective Bonner looked at his wife with questioning eyes while at the same time pulling her toward the T.V. room. The T.V. room was connected to the living room. The living room had no divider between it and the kitchen. Julie had preferred the open concept and now it came in handy. She wanted to keep an eye on the kids, but she needed to talk to her husband. NOW!

Julie pointed to the rose laying on the table. He looked at her, but he still did not understand what she was trying to tell him.

"Bob, this rose was tacked to our front door when the kids and I got home from mothers. It also had this note placed behind it."

The detective took the note from his wife. In bold letters it said, "She's Mine." It was also underlined three times.

"Bob, what is going on? Didn't Chloe get a red rose from her stalker?"

"Yes, Julie. I'm afraid she did. I'm not sure what's happening, but I'm pretty sure someone is telling me to back off," the detective answered. He remained silent for a moment and then began again.

"I finished my report on Chloe's case today. That's why I stayed late. I finished the official report shortly after everyone left, but I wanted to make copies of all the written reports after everyone was gone. What I couldn't get in the copier earlier I saved until after work. That old Polaroid I keep in my desk sure came in handy. Now I have all the information I need. All I have to do is go through the file one more time and write down anything extra that comes to my mind. Hold on, Julie." Detective Bonner stopped, walked toward the kitchen, then breathed a sigh relief when his eyes fell on the folder they had just been discussing.

"I have a confession to make," the detective said, as he returned to the room Julie was in. "I know you remember when you, Seth, Chloe and me, were all standing in the squad room after saying our goodbyes."

"Yes, Bob. I remember. Please, get to the point."

"The three of you had said your goodbyes. While I was standing there, the hairs on the back of my neck stood up. I couldn't believe it. It was the same way I felt, when I had the feeling someone was watching me after the death of Sean Delaney."

"You were in the squad room. I'm sure there were several men watching us say our goodbyes."

"I know. But this feeling was not a good feeling. I can't explain it. When I looked at Chloe, I knew she had felt the same thing, because she had turned pale. I guess we both decided to ignore it. We were in a police station. Of all places this is where you should be safe. But now, I guess I should have paid more attention. Although I guess I did, in a way."

"How's that?"

"I made all those copies. I knew things weren't adding up, but I didn't know why. Then there was the pressure to close the case, but at least I know I was on the right track."

"I'm sorry, Julie. I was trying to protect you and the kids and I ended up scaring you."

Just as Bob finished speaking, the car alarm went off in the detective's official vehicle. Thankful that he had not taken his gun off when he had come through the front door, he headed outside telling Julie to lock the door behind him.

"What's going on, Mom?" Bobby Jr. asked his mother.

"The alarm on your dad's car went off and he went to check it out."

"I'm scared, Mommy!" Tiffany cried.

"It's okay, Tiffany." Julie cradled her daughter in her arms while at the same time moving to stand by her son.

"If you two are finished eating, maybe you'd like to watch some T.V."

"Mom, you don't let us watch T.V. this late." Bobby Jr. said.

"I know." She whispered to him, "but if you'll take Tiffany into the other room maybe it will calm her down. That would be a big help right now."

"Come on, Tiffany. I'll watch with you," Bobby Jr. told his little sister. Julie sat her daughter down and smiled as she dutifully followed her older brother into the living room.

"Thanks, Bobby Jr. I appreciate your help." Julie said, smiling to herself. She knew he was scared, too. She just didn't want to make a big issue out of it. Heck, she was scared, too.

"Julie, let me in." Detective Bonner said, as he knocked at the door.

"Is everything okay, Bob?"

"Everything is fine, Julie."

"Everything is not fine. Now, is not the time to be keeping me in the dark. I can't protect myself or the kids if I don't know what is going on."

"I know you're right Julie. I just don't know what's going on myself." He stopped for a moment and then continued, "When I pulled in the driveway, I grabbed the pizzas and then shut and locked the door behind me like always. I don't know what anyone could have been after."

Both Julie and her husband went to the kitchen table. There, right before their eyes, lay the file.

"Bob," Julie said, "Could it be the file? Could someone have been after that?"

"It could be. I guess I laid the file on top of the pizzas when I brought them into the house. I didn't even pay any attention to what I was doing."

"Are we okay, Dad?" Bobby Jr. asked, quietly walking up to stand behind his dad.

"We're fine, son."

Julie went in to check on their daughter, but she was fully entranced by her favorite show "Frozen". Julie returned to the kitchen. When she did, she stared into her husband's eyes. She knew her husband well enough to know he was worried.

The man watched as Detective Bonner came outside to see why his alarm had gone off. He had hoped the detective had left the file in the car, but it must have been on top of the boxes of pizza.

He had also been watching when the detective's wife had returned home and found the note and the rose on the door. In fact, if she had gotten there just a few minutes earlier, she would have caught him in the act.

He had accomplished what he had set out to do. Now it was time to return to Chloe's house, but as he looked around he realized that it was getting dark. He had been so engrossed in what he was doing he had let the darkness creep up on him undetected. He decided he would go home, get some sleep and then return to the woods behind Chloe's house in the morning.

Seth had gone to work this morning free from the fear that something might happen to Chloe while he was gone. His boss and good friend, Calvin, had bent over backwards to help him. Technology had been a blessing for a lot of Seth's work could be accomplished at home and when it couldn't, he simply went in to the office. Technology helped him keep his job. But good friends, well that was even better.

Chloe had finished her "God Time" this morning, but she continued to sit and enjoy the outdoors. As she sat there quietly, she began to go over what she and Seth had been through. The fact three different men had stalked her was unbelievable. She was deep in thought when the phone rang.

"Chloe, this is Julie. Would you like to meet somewhere and have lunch today?"

"Sounds great. Where would you like to meet?"

"How about the S&S Cafe?"

"That sounds great." Chloe jumped up and hurried to the bedroom to get ready.

Chloe arrived at the S&S Cafe right at eleven. As she pulled into a parking space, she knew that from all the cars it was going to be a very busy place this morning. She saw Julie's car and knew she must have gotten here pretty early to have gotten one so close. Once she located Julie, she walked over to her table and sat down.

"Hi, Julie. It's good to see you. It looks like I have a while to wait so why don't you go ahead and eat and I'll go get mine whenever the line gets a little shorter. We can talk a little bit while I'm waiting." Chloe said, with a smile on her face.

"I really am glad you called. I've missed you."

"I've missed you, too, Chloe. It seems longer than just last… Hi, Bob. Come sit with us." Julie said, with a guilty look on her face.

"Hi, Chloe. Hi, Julie. I can't stay long," he said, as he sat down beside his wife.

"Okay, you two. What's going on? It's no accident that Bob showed up not long after I did. Is it?"

Julie looked at her friend a little sheepishly as her husband began to talk.

"No, Chloe. It's not. I asked Julie to call and set this up. I didn't want you to be alone after our talk. So…"

"Bob, stop. Just tell me what is going on."

Detective Bonner started with his feeling at the station then he told her about making an extra file. He told her about Julie finding the red rose with a note tacked under it on their front door. On the note were the words "She's Mine."

"Chloe, I really don't know what is going on."

"What you're telling me, Bob. Or at least what I think you are telling me is that I have a fourth stalker. Is that right? And how can that be? It's not even logical."

"I didn't want to wait until this evening to tell you, but I would like for you to go through the files. Would you like to go to the station? I thought maybe you might think of something you had not thought of before. What do you think?"

"I don't want to do it at the station."

"Why not?"

Chloe repeated what she had felt the last time she had been there. And I was pretty sure you felt it, too."

"I did. It was just as hard for me to believe."

"I couldn't either so I just ignored it."

"Is there any way you and Seth can come over for dinner tonight? Maybe you can take a look at the files then."

"I do have some errands I can run, but I don't feel like being by myself."

"Well, why don't I go with you." Julie said with concern.

"Thanks Julie. I appreciate it, but…"

"No, buts. Let's eat then we can decide what to do."

Chloe went to get her sandwich while Detective Bonner and Julie said goodbye. She picked up her sandwich and as she returned to Julie's table, she passed the detective on his way out.

"Thanks, Bob, for letting me know what's going on. Could you call Seth for me?"

"Sure, Chloe. No problem," and off he went.

Chloe returned to the table and sat down beside Julie. For a while, they talked about light hearted subjects, but then it was time to decide what they were going to do.

"I think I have a solution. Tiffany is my mother's. Why don't I have her pick up Bobby Jr.? I love my kids, but I think this is one time when we don't need any distractions."

"I agree," Chloe was relieved for she hadn't wanted to be by herself anyway.

Both women stood and walked in the direction of the door. Julie stopped to talk to someone she knew while Chloe kept walking in the direction of her car. When she got there, she opened the door and was in the process of throwing her purse on the passenger's seat when she saw the red rose.

"I can't take this anymore," she thought to herself. "God, do You hear me? I can't take this anymore." As she stood staring at the red rose, she began to cry.

After talking to her friends, Julie had gone to her car. She looked for Chloe to let her know she was ready to go. She found her just standing there looking into her car.

"Chloe, are you alright?" Julie called out, but her friend didn't answer. She stood there as if she hadn't even heard her. When Chloe made no move to get in her car, Julie decided she better go check on her.

"Chloe, are you alright?" Julie said, as she approached her car. When she saw the look on Chloe's face, she looked in the same direction Chloe was staring and she too saw the red rose.

"Oh, no. Chloe." Julie said, as she pulled her cell phone out of her pocket and called her husband. Detective Bonner got up from his desk and ran toward the S&S Café. He knew exactly where to find them because they had not moved from when he had been there earlier.

Julie stood beside Chloe as they waited for Bob to return. Which didn't take long, because the station was close by.

"Julie, why don't you take Chloe home with you now. I'll take care of this and call Seth since I haven't had the chance to call him yet." The detective said, on his arrival at Chloe's car.

"I'm glad you're here, Bob." Julie said looking at her husband. And with a slight push on Chloe's back, the two friends headed in the direction of Julie's car.

"Thanks, Julie. I don't know what I would have done without you."

"That's what friends are for, Chloe."

CHAPTER 32

The man watched from his car not far from where Chloe was parked. He had gone in at the same time Chloe and Julie were coming out. He had even held the door open for them. A quick hello and they had been on their way. He had been sitting at a table by the window when Chloe reached her car. He had been so engrossed in what was taking place outside, he failed to hear them tell him his order was ready. After calling him twice, they just brought it to him since he had been there many times before.

The man watched intently as Chloe got in Julie's car and they left. He watched Detective Bonner talking on his cell phone and in just a few minutes Dave from Forensics was there. Detective Bonner explained what he wanted and then left. The man was certainly pleased with himself with all the commotion he had caused.

Seth was on his way home from work. It had felt good to be able to go to work, do his job and then come home in the evening to Chloe. Just a normal everyday life was a blessing. One he was thoroughly enjoying. Then Seth's cell phone rang.

"Isn't it about time for you to give up. I would hate for you to die trying to save her. Just give up. Let go." The man said, while Seth listened in stunned silence.

Seth pulled over to the side of the road. His hands were shaking so bad he could hardly hold onto his phone. So he dropped it in the seat beside him.

When he heard those words, Seth put his head on the steering wheel and let loose of all the emotions he had been holding in for so long. He felt guilty because when he heard those words give up, he knew he had wanted to, but he also knew, he and Chloe were a team. He loved her and he would never leave her. They would fight this problem together and with God on their side, they would win. He just knew it.

Seth bowed his head while he silently said a little prayer. "Oh, Lord, my God. I know You are on our side. I just don't understand how there can be four stalkers. How can that even be possible?"

Seth continued to pray as he pulled back out on to "59" heading north.

Once again his cell phone rang, but this time it was Detective Bonner. The first thing Detective Bonner told him was that Chloe was alright. The next was that Chloe was over at his house and they were going to discuss what had just happened after he got there.

After talking to Detective Bonner, Seth prayed all the harder. He talked to God as if God was sitting in the seat beside Him. He also mused to himself how people would probably laugh at him for this whole conversation he was having. He didn't care. It was just a fleeting thought that passed through his head as he continued praying. He only stopped when he pulled into the detective's driveway.

"How are you holding up, Seth?" Detective Bonner asked, as he waited for Seth to walk up beside him.

"Your call was a big downer, but otherwise I'm okay." Seth answered. The two men shook hands and proceeded to walk toward the front door.

Julie's mother picked up the kids and took them over to her house. Everyone needed to be able to give their undivided attention toward the problem. Julie and Chloe had made some coffee and sandwiches, but no one really felt like eating. They sat there trying to have a little small talk before everyone got down to business. It didn't work.

"Okay, let's get this over with." Seth said. "I can't relax and I'm not very hungry."

Detective Bonner reached over and grabbed the folder from the couch beside him. He placed it on the table.

"We probably need to let Chloe look at it first to see if something pops out. When she finishes with a paper, she can pass it on." Detective Bonner said. He began to scatter the papers in front of him then he changed his mind.

"I think we probably need to move to the kitchen table. We'll have more room there."

"Before we get started, I have something to add to your notes." Seth said. Everyone stood and headed in the direction of the kitchen. Each one had something in their hands. Detective Bonner had most of the contents of the file. Seth proceeded to tell them about the phone call and what had been said.

"Seth, I am so sorry."

Detective Bonner wrote down everything that Seth told them. He felt as if Seth was holding something back and it bothered him. The four of them continued to pour over the papers until they were blue in the face.

"Why don't we take a break? Everything seems to be running together before my eyes." Chloe said, as she turned toward the couch to go sit down.

"I know you're right, Chloe. Why don't we go sit out on the patio? I hate to stop, but maybe we'll have a fresh perspective when we come back."

"That's sounds great, Julie. Can we go out to the little alcove. I just love sitting out there. When I'm there I feel as if we are in our own special place. Like the Garden of Eden."

Little did they know, Satan had entered the little alcove just as he had done in the Garden of Eden two thousand plus years ago.

This alcove was also Julie's favorite place. It wasn't all that far from the men sitting on the patio. It was also a quiet place where she and Chloe could talk without the men being able to hear what they were saying.

"Julie, I love this little alcove. Remote, but not too remote." Chloe said, as she and Julie sat down in the double swing. "I really like what you've done to this little area."

Julie had added two chairs on either side of the swing, but each one was facing toward the small table in the middle. The chairs were oversized with large pillows placed on the bottom and in the back. Julie had also placed large pillows on the swing.

"I could just sink into these pillows and stay here forever."

They continued their small talk for a few minutes, but then Chloe said, "Julie, what am I going to do? I can't go on this way forever. We can't."

"As you went over the files, did anything catch your attention?"

"Not really. Well, yes, it did. It seemed that no matter where we went, a stalker was there. I also can't get over the fact that both Bob and I felt something in the squad room. How can that be? In the squad room of all places."

"Hold on, Chloe. I need to ask Bob something?" Julie got up and went over to where their husbands were sitting. She was only gone for a few minutes, but when she got back Chloe was gone.

"Bob, Chloe's gone!" Julie screamed.

Immediately Detective Bonner picked up his cell phone and called the station alerting the dispatcher of Chloe's disappearance. Since he knew a couple of officers that lived right down the road, he called them for backup.

Seth headed for the woods, but Detective Bonner called him back.

"Seth, it's dark out there. You're only going to get yourself lost or killed. One or the other. After several minutes Detective Bonner came running back.

"I have an idea. Seth, meet me at my car. I'll run and get my keys."

Detective Bonner took a couple of minutes to find his keys. And Julie was yelling she was going, too. All three met at Detective Bonner's car, which he unlocked, and then all three piled in.

"What are you thinking, Bob?" Seth asked.

"Where did the other two stalkers take Chloe?"

"To the Delaney house." both Julie and Seth said in unison.

CHAPTER 33

"**D**etective Roberts, why are you doing this?" Chloe asked, as she desperately tried to keep from crying.

"Get out of the car, Chloe. NOW!"

"This is the Delaney house. Why are we here?"

"I'll explain after we get inside."

Chloe walked into the living room, but then headed toward the kitchen. Detective Roberts was guiding her with his gun hand.

"No, I think we'll go to the observation room. You do remember the observation room. Don't you, Chloe?"

Chloe remained quiet as the detective pushed her down the hall. He opened the door and gave her a shove. She stumbled and almost fell.

"What do you want?"

"You."

"Why me?"

"It is sort of funny although you probably won't think so. It started out as a game my brothers wanted to play. One of my brothers saw you at the Mexican restaurant. They had played the game before. One of them would pick someone, then they would hire someone to do the stalking and they would just watch."

"But somewhere along the way Clay decided otherwise. In the beginning, Sean and Clay would take turns watching as John Bledsoe did the stalking. Since Sean and Clay were twins, so to speak, they could alternate at the job in the restaurant plus they could alternate watching you and no one would be the wiser. To make a long story short, Sean changed the plan and he died. Your incessant praying was the catalyst. It turned everyone against everyone else. It turned out it wasn't about you anymore. It was a war against God. And now, God is going to lose." Detective Roberts reached up and pulled some additions off his face. "I was burned in a fire several years ago so these additions were added to make my face more appealing."

Chloe could only stare in recognition at the smiling face before her.

"Triplets."

Seeing the expression on her face the man could not help but laugh. "I really tried to go straight once I got out of the pen, but my brothers needed my help. I paid someone for a new identity and ended up working in the police department. Ironic, huh?"

Chloe listened while the answers to all her questions were revealed. Actually, there was no true answer, for it had been random. One paid, three related. There was no rhyme or reason to any of this. Nothing she had done or didn't do had caused this.

Her thoughts came to a sudden end as she saw Detective Robert's raise his gun and hit her beside the head. She stumbled, but this time she couldn't keep herself from falling to the floor.

"My brothers are dead because of you." He looked at her with deadly eyes.

Detective Roberts raised his gun and pointed it right at her.

"Lord, show me the way out of here." Chloe said. "I'm yours no matter which way this goes." Chloe stood up, shut her eyes and waited.

"Bang! Bang, Bang!" Chloe heard the shots, but felt nothing.

When Detective Roberts and Chloe weren't in the kitchen, Detective Bonner immediately headed toward the room they called the observation room. He could hear the police sirens, but he knew he couldn't wait. Chloe's life was in danger. She needed help and she needed it now.

Just as the police arrived, everyone outside heard the shots. Both Seth and Julie stood silent and still. They were afraid. They didn't want to know the outcome of the shots they had just heard. But then they were both on the move. Not even thinking, they headed toward the sound. One of the officers tried to stop them, but he didn't succeed.

When Detective Bonner entered the room, Detective Roberts turned and pointed his gun directly at him. Thankfully, Chloe decided right at that moment to open her eyes. She didn't have time to think. She just bent over and once again used her head butt maneuver. She had done it on Sean and now she was going to repeat it on Detective Roberts.

Detective Robert's gun was pointed right at Detective Bonner so instead of aiming her head at the detective's stomach she aimed it at his back. When Chloe's 'head butt' connected with Detective Robert's back, it made his shot go wild missing Detective Bonner by inches. Getting the upper hand, Detective Bonner shot Detective Roberts twice. He fell to the floor and didn't get up.

"Thanks, Chloe." Detective Bonner said, stepping over the detective's body. He bent over and took Chloe's hand to help her up. She had been knocked off balanced after coming in contact with the detective's body.

"No, Bob. Thank you..." Chloe didn't finish her sentence because her eyes spotted Seth as he arrived at the doorway and right behind him, she spotted Julie.

"Chloe, are you alright?" Seth asked as she stepped into his arms.

Julie pushed past Seth and stopped directly in front of her husband.

"Julie, you didn't stay outside like I told you to."

"Nope, I sure didn't, but I did let Seth go first." Julie said putting her arms around her husband.

After a couple of seconds, Detective Bonner told everyone, "Everybody out. This is a crime scene."

It didn't take long for the room to empty out. It was now his crime scene. It was pretty cut and dry, but a certain protocol had to be followed with a shooting. And this time they would close this case. Chloe's case.

Epilogue

"Chloe." Detective Bonner said, as the four of them sat eating hamburgers on the Bonner's patio. "I need to ask you a question?"

"Sure, Bob, what is it?"

Chloe had been talking to Julie, but when Detective Bonner called her name, she turned around to face him.

"Did you feel anything? Anything at all when we left the Delaney's house."

"No, Bob. I didn't feel a thing. Did you?"

"No, I didn't. And I'm really glad you didn't either. Now let's eat."

After saying a short prayer for God taking care of them and then blessing the food, the four of them started joking around enjoying the gift they had been given. Life.

The kids were playing in the yard and the adults sat on the patio watching.

"I have an announcement to make." Chloe said, smiling. "Seth and I are going to have a baby."

"Oh, Chloe. That's wonderful." Julie said.

"Aunt Chloe, men don't have babies. Do they dad?" Bobby Jr. asked. As children so often do, they hear things you don't realize they hear.

"No, Bobby Jr. they don't. Now go play with your sister."

"We are so happy for you two."

"God is so good." Chloe said.

"All the time." Julie answered.

The wind that had been so still, suddenly rustled through the trees. The four of them looked startled for a moment then they looked at each other and laughed. They quickly bowed their heads and with a quick heartfelt thank you to God, they returned to their hamburgers with gusto. Chloe couldn't help it as her eyes drifted in the direction of the trees one last time. As she did, the trees once again began to blow.

GOD IS, WAS, AND WILL
FOREVER BE GOOD!

Poems From the Heart

9781937911614 (soft cover)
9781937911621 (hard cover)
9781937911669 (ebook)

The decision to follow Jesus is the most important decision of your life. I pray that as you read the enclosed poems, they will cause you to seek a deeper relationship with Him.

She's Mine

9781937911614 (soft cover)
9781937911621 (hard cover)
9781937911669 (ebook)

Chloe kept trying to pull free, but the person that held her under the water had his hands entangled in her hair and she couldn't get away. Darkness threatened but still she tried. And then, nothing.

GOD Things

9781937911959 (soft cover)
9781937911966 (hard cover)

So as we go about our day,
And we give credit to the Lord above.
We find it is in all those little "God Things".
That we are woven together with His love.

Silent and Still

9781937911973 (soft cover)
9781937911980 (hard cover)
9781937911997 (ebook)

The man was already in place when the sun came up the next morning. He stood by his favorite tree smiling to himself as he watched the back of the house. He had come up with the most brilliant plan, or so he thought, and he couldn't wait to put it into action.

Meet the Author

La Johna Newbould

is a late-in-life Christian. It wasn't until she was in her early forties that she accepted Jesus Christ as her Lord and Savior. Once again she feels led to publish two more books. So with a total of four, she steps forward in faith, believing that anyone who reads any one of them will chose to have a relationship with Jesus one step at a time. For everyone has to begin somewhere.